The Dragonfly Fling

The Dragonfly Fling

Jean McKay

Coach House Press

Toronto

Published with the assistance of the Canada Council,
the Ontario Arts Council, and the Ontario Ministry of
Culture and Communications.

Canadian Cataloguing in Publication Data

McKay, Jean, 1943-
  The dragonfly fling

ISBN 0-88910-438-7

1. Title.

PS8575.K38D7 1992   C813'.54   C92-093318-
1PR9199.3.M35D7 1992

Gentle and just pleasure
It is, being human, to have won from space
This unchill, habitable interior

Margaret Avison

Acknowledgments

A few of these stories appeared in *The Malahat Review* and the University of Western Ontario *Gazette*.

Thanks to the Group: Beryl Baylis, Daryll Kaufmann, Kathie Lambert and Philip Ireland, for their safe houses; to Don Gutteridge and Leon Rooke, for their timely encouragement; to John Ireland, for the use of his name; and, of course, to Sal and Joe, my best pairs of eyeballs.

Financial assistance from the Ontario Arts Council facilitated the writing of some of these stories.

Contents

Grab your honey

There's nothing for it but to begin. Bring out your drums, your zithers, your cream cheese folded-over sandwiches, and let's see if we can scare up a little dancing. Let's tune up the lute, snap the lid off that five-gallon bucket of bread-and-butter pickles, find the condoms, and get on with it.

There's old Mozart, *he* doesn't wish he was dead.

He *is* dead, of course, but that belongs to a different ideological ring in this multi-ring circus.

A girl in a cherry-coloured coat runs across a snowy neighbouring backyard, past the yellow brick side wall of her house, and disappears.

The brick, until recently, was warming itself in the late-morning crisp winter sun; ten minutes ago it would have registered the light moth-crossing of her shadow, but now the sky has clouded over. She runs, in her cherry-coloured coat, and disappears.

So let's not lose any time.

Let's not say Point of Order, Point of Interest, or In Conclusion. Let's not discuss the bottom line.

Let no holds be barred.

from the Dragonfly Notebook

The Raw Materials (pinned to the wall, accumulating at random):

1. Harley-Davidson cigarette packages. Black and gold. Can't you see this beautiful black and gold dragonfly, suspended from the ceiling?

HARLEY'S BEST: FUCK THE REST

I get them from a woman at work. Somebody smuggles them over the border for her.

2. Plastic shrink-wrap from a bike lock. It's already looking like an abdominal carapace even with nothing at all done to it. It will become a dung beetle, pushing up its shit-ball sun to the surface of the desert.

I plan to be a dung beetle when I finally get rid of this particular mortal coil. I've had my requisition in for years, in triplicate, with impeccable references. In order to ensure that they don't just file it away and forget about it, I send a memo every few months to remind them, keeping it hot. *Please, sirs, or madams; please, you-all, next I want to be a dung beetle.* They owe it to me, and they know they do, after sending me down with this. Good legs, ridiculous hair, a penchant for needlepoint and the naming of cats. Less well-equipped than the Boy Scouts.

I DON'T KNOW HOW I'M SUPPOSED TO DO ANYTHING WITH THIS GODDAMN TOY SHOVEL

3. Twenty-seven newspaper clippings of a chef. I'll have to be careful of the glue, the ink from the back will leak through and obliterate his eyeballs. I want the wings to be a pastiche, a chorus, a clamour, a pealing, a veritable ratatouille of his eyeballs. Eyeball upon eyeball.

An elephant killed a boy last week. I know so many stories of that one big story. Boy gets to know elephant well, becomes his friend, there's a condition of mutual trust, and then, one sunny afternoon, the elephant smucks him.

Too bad.

How does God keep track? Maybe he's computerized. They've put St. Peter out to pasture, hired a hotshot from the Harvard business school.

4. A standard pasteboard egg carton. This will be
the many-humped dragonfly, the dinosaur dragonfly, now extinct because he was too heavy to
fly. How many times did he try, and crash into a
crater, into a mountainside, into a tree?

Smuck, smuck, smuck, youth brains splay out under
elephant feet, is that cherry-coated girl safely indoors
with her cocoa, or did she get scooped up out front by two
nondescript men in a beige '72 Chevrolet? Are they
butchering her this very minute in a culvert in Nissourri
Township? Her own warm vibrant blood would put the
cherry coat to shame.
It's that kind of morning, all right.

5. A single bee, a yellow-jacket; under the glass it
took him twenty-four hours to die. He stung me in
the leg, in my own kitchen, in the privacy of my
own kitchen, AS THEY SAY (oh why did Graham
Chapman have to die, I hope it short-circuited that
Harvard business school dick-head's computer;
some goods are just too hot to handle), I ripped off
my jeans in response to the pain, hopped around
the kitchen in my underwear trying to discover
what it was, found him spinning on the floor,
popped a glass over him, left him to die.

I'm a nice girl, really, when I see a group of flossies admiring the baby I always engage the older child on some totally unrelated topic, that's the sort of girl I usually am, but I left the glass over this yellow-jacket to kill him, with nary a thought for his slow death.

Well. Not true. With *many* thoughts for his slow death. With this very slow death, on my own kitchen floor, with my two cats, well-named, circling, eyeing him, or snoozing, their paws coyly tucked beneath their plump breasts; with this death, I say, I wanted to attack Death Himself, I wanted to attack the widening circle of steamy buffalo shit I once stepped in at Riding Mountain National Park, as the sun was going down, and I was pouring the scotch before it was too dark to see, so we could sit on the picnic table in the knifing prairie wind and watch the kids' faces as they poked at the fire.

Every second, an elephant kills a youth; how power ful a dragonfly will it have to be, with this slow-deathed yellow-jacket forming its central eyeball, to compensate for that?

I don't want Graham Chapman dead, or John Donne, or Glenn Gould, or my father. I'll send out this dragonfly, this bee-eyed concentrate of anti-death dragonfly to stitch through the world, shroud up death and cart him, spitting venom, to the ultimate landfill centre of nothing.

Survival

Waking up in the dark, on a beach, stomach down in the sand, feet and legs still in the water, I must have made it this far and passed out. No stars, total blackness, I hitch forward on my belly, hands out front, scanning the sand, sweeping for danger, forward again, my feet are out of the water now, sweep, hitch, sweep, hitch, my left hand strikes something large. I grab it in both hands. Large and leathery. Like an elephant's ear. Holes in it, I find two close together, two more, another two, there seems to be a symmetry, then one large wide one, my fingers explore inside, and I suddenly recognize teeth. This is a head. Not a skull, a head. There's skin, not dried, not rotting, but this head isn't conscious. I've had my fingers in its nose, its ears, its eyes, oh god, two of those holes were eyes, why didn't they squirt? Birds must have plucked out the eyeballs. Or rats. I go back to the teeth. I want to kiss the mouth, lick the teeth, I rub my fingers over them, in the dark they're large as mountain ranges. I put one arm around the head, cradle my other hand into the teeth, settle my body full length into the sand, and fall asleep.

Mushroom

Beryl put a mushroom in the centre of the table.

'Open yourself up to it,' she said.

We all contemplated the mushroom, our jaws grinding relentlessly on the rubbery jujubes. Everybody had their favourite colour jube, except for the martyr. She had the colour she hated most; so everybody was happy.

It was a warm rainy night, the first day of February. Abortion had just been legalized, there was a major oil spill on the West Coast, the woman in Kincardine who was accused of murdering her baby had had her preliminary hearing that afternoon.

But we weren't thinking about any of this. We were sucking jubes, looking at the mushroom, waiting for something to happen.

Our vicious guard dog was sleeping like a baby under the table, whimpering occasionally. The toilet tank was running, but none of us wanted to break the circle to fix it.

Jube juice squirted through our teeth. The flickering candles drew us closer in on ourselves, closer in on the mushroom.

17

The mushroom was upside down. Beryl had put it there, on the glass table in the centre of the room. The curve of its cap arced against the curve of its reflection, two milky half-moons.

Open ourselves up to it.

Something wasn't working. We were being blocked. Maybe the dog dreams were too powerful. Maybe the rain-filled air around the little house wasn't clear enough.

Whatever the reason, the mushroom remained, on the table, upside down, merely a mushroom. The candles guttered, the toilet sighed, we ran clean out of jubes.

Atrophy was beginning to set in. We could hear each other swallow.

We gave up.

Then, of course, it happened. The toilet stopped running, and the mushroom began to rock slowly back and forth. It gathered speed, began to roll, careened around the table, hit a candle, and bounced off into the mouth of the vicious guard dog who had just awakened and was yawning. He gulped, yelped, spit it out with such force that it hit the wall, drove straight through, out into the wet February evening, shot like a bullet down Big Simcoe Street and lodged in the left ear of the already hard-of-hearing Vietnamese proprietor of the Big V variety store.

Lineage

Do ancestors have to be dead?

Of course not. In fact, some of them have yet to be born, to supply the missing question for the answers we can only partially frame.

Ice-storm

The ice makes my mother ecstatic. 'Isn't it beautiful?' she says over the phone. 'Each little branch and twig is outlined in gold. With the sun shining on it, it just sparkles! Like angels' wings!'

God has brought this to her, beauty that still proves He cares about His world. Her old, tired God that I first met in the fifties, when He wanted me to keep my knees together and wear hats to church. When His body was cubes of white bread, and His blood tasted like Welch's grape juice. My son, watching communion glasses pass through a congregation in a TV movie the other night said, 'Do they ever use real blood?' With an outsider's point of view, he would like it to make some visceral sense. He's never taken communion. He's never sat in church, smelling the varnish, itching and twitching until he could get out, and home, and into some real clothes. It's a part of my childhood I chose to spare him. It wasn't a hard decision.

But to my mother, this is a direct gift. The old boy has roused Himself, rolled over, pointed His finger and sent down this ice especially for her. I can hear, in her voice over the phone, how she's quivering with excitement. I feel the old sense of embarrassment, that something this unbridled and inane is being aired in public. Over the telephone lines. My mind flashes down the single strand of wire, wrapped into its insulated bundle, that connects her living-room to mine. I wonder if a driver, idling at the stoplight at Oxford and Wharncliffe, looks up to see that flash of shameless foolishness pulsing along through the coating of ice.

I no longer ask, but what about cancer/Bangladesh/ war/the girl in my son's high school with no arms? The old argument is as tired as God Himself. We've long since played that one out. He works in mysterious ways. I snorted, and slammed doors.

I capitulate now, as easily as I'll take McDonald's over Burger King, even though I prefer Burger King's french fries. It means that little to me anymore.

'Yes,' I say. 'It really is beautiful.'

'God has sent this ice directly to Grandma,' I tell my son.

He says, 'It's only weather.'

What the ice *has* done is kill my maple tree. I bought it two springs ago, when I moved into this house, at the beginning of my however belated New Life. Taking my first steps away from the smoking crater of my bombed-out marriage. I planted the tree to tell myself that time is reliable. That these fragmented chunks of shock, of pain, of not being able to find the toilet paper in the middle of the night in this alien bathroom would eventually settle, sort themselves into a pattern. That if I waited long enough I would be able to look back on a new past.

The first spring it grew 17 leaves. Last spring it had 158. I marked these statistics up on the front doorjamb in pencil, the way I used to mark my children's increasing height. This spring, I thought, there'll be too many to count. It will have declared itself a tree. I'll be okay.

I look at it out the window, at its small collection of torn branches piled around its feet. It's a stick again. One upright stick. It looks just like it did when I bought it, with the addition of wounds.

My son puts his hand on my shoulder and says, again, 'It's only weather.'

Aquarium

For a while, Esther Williams was my childhood hero. At
the same time that my favourite male was Jerry Lewis.
That was the trouble with the standard fifties upbringing,
it didn't give you any information on the signals of sexu-
ality, so you couldn't recognize energy when you saw it.
Or, conversely, you invested or imagined a lot of energy
into ludicrous stuffed-doll images like Esther Williams.
Swimming about, swimming about, coming out to cry, or
just generally agonize, swimming about again, coming
out finally to kiss some jerk with a crew cut. The end.

For a while, it was Dale Evans. That rubbed off from
a horsey friend of mine, who wanted to be a cowgirl. She
had white jeans and a whip. She put on her white jeans
and stood in her backyard and practised cracking her
whip, to see if she could hit the fence. Any asshole could
have hit the fence. Whip-cracking isn't all that demanding.

Her parents owned a C-grade rambling hotel on
Georgian Bay, and they took me up with them once for a
Thanksgiving weekend when they closed it down for the
winter. My friend and I combed the sand during the day

and found about five dollars each in lost change. In the
evening we all played poker, and her folks were worried
that my folks would think it was sinful. I'd never heard of
poker. I didn't know if it was on my parents' sin list or not.
I used the five bucks I'd made on the beach, and parleyed
it into another five. Came home with ten bucks, at a time
when my allowance was fifteen cents a week. Ten bucks
was the price of two music lessons at the Royal Conser-
vatory. In short, a lot of money.

When we got back to my place, my friend's mother
came in with me and told my folks I'd been playing poker,
and that if they were going to be mad at anybody it should
be at her, rather than me, since she let me do it. They said
polite and friendly things. It was some big adult joke that
seemed to mean it was okay for me to sin as long as the
grownups thought it was funny.

I went to bed, and lay there, looking at my full-colour
pin-up of Esther Williams, and knew in my heart that she
would never play poker. The next day I gave the whole
ten bucks to the church organ fund.

So I had it both ways. I got the thrill of sinning, albeit
retroactive, and a great deal of attention for being virtu-
ous. Giving up all that money, though, made me feel kind
of sick. Grey, like a swimmer who's been in the water for
just too long.

The Family,
in the Elmwood Branch
Family Restaurant

This morning I watched a total stranger scramble my breakfast eggs. EGGS COOKED IN FRONT OF YOUR EYES, the sign said. The cook was very deft, with his little Teflon pan and wooden paddle. Nice finely-cut blue eyes.

At the table we fell to telling stories of people who nervously joggle their legs up and down. My mother began, digging back, what, sixty-eight years, to a boy who sat across the aisle from her in Math class. He joggled his leg, and his feet smelled, and the joggling seemed to spread the stench. So the smell comes back to her now whenever anyone joggles.

I told about poor Mrs. Hardisty, grade eleven French teacher, last class Friday afternoons in a crowded portable. She stood in front of our row and we all joggled, and bounced her over to the next row, who joggled her back. We passed her about the front of the room like a rubber doll. She was too embarrassed to admit it was happening, so she couldn't do anything to stop it.

The eggs didn't taste any different, cooked in front of our eyes or not.

Then my brother told a story of our father's, Chemistry class this time, the teacher at the front measuring out minute amounts of chemicals onto a finely balanced scale. The class all joggled at once, the powders sifted off the scales onto the table, the teacher couldn't figure out why.

Me again, about how great hulking Ian used to feed tiny baby Jessica her bottle, his leg joggling her head and the bottle both up and down. Her tiny moist mouth holding onto the rubber nipple for dear life. 'Ian,' we said. 'Stop joggling before you snap that child's head clean off.'

More coffee from the waitress.

Then my niece, Debra. When Gord's brother died. He disappeared through the ice, skidoo and all, into a dark northern lake. Debra sat on the floor at the memorial service, her elbow resting on another girl's knee, both of them crying, the other girl joggling. No body for them to focus on, only the memory of the black gaping water in all their minds. And now, when she sits in History class, the boys on either side joggle to get her mad. She doesn't want to tell them about Gord's brother. Only wants to flail at them, rip out their throats with her bare hands.

Skipping

Once I went through puberty, my mother said I had to stop skipping. The sacred little home that God has put inside you, she said, for a baby to grow in, could be injured. It's loose in there, and it might jar, or get tipped, so you wouldn't be able to have children.

Growing up was all like that. Finally, after ten years of watching me be Daddy's girl, learning to box, tail-saw, shingle a roof, crack a hardball right over the school, she could move in and say Welcome To Womanhood: here's a list of four thousand things you'll never do again. She had me, Gretel, in her cage. She was, bless her, inside the cage herself, but back then neither of us knew that.

My father gave up. For some reason he thought she was right, and I saw myself floating away from him and his real world to an island exile, trapped forever peeling carrots in church basements, cleaning toilets, doing my duty in bed. This separation from my father, while he stood silently by and let it happen, was far worse for me than his eventual death.

But, miraculously, skipping was one place where he

held firm. He insisted that it was safe. I sat on the landing and listened down the back stairs to them arguing it out in the kitchen.

'It's not going to do her any harm,' he said. 'Look at all the professional women athletes who do things far more active than skipping.'

They talked about tissues, integuments, muscles and their attachments. I'll give them this: they both knew their anatomy. I leaned back against the stairs and hauled up my shirt so I could look at my belly while they argued, wishing it had a window in it like a washing-machine door so I could see what they were talking about.

He won, and I went on skipping. But her final word had a sinister ring.

'I can't help it,' she said, choking on a sob, 'I just keep thinking about what happened to Grandma!'

What did happen to Grandma? They didn't discuss it. My belly and I stared at each other in terror.

Homunculus

It's bulbous, like a beet-root, like carrots gone wrong, all warty and horny down there under the dirt. It's the fat little tuber that starts a new world.

'Did you stop the paper, stop the mail, take the cats to the kennel? And who's got the homunculus?'

Jenny's got it. She's put it in the trunk with the watermelon, and propped the baby's blanket between them so they won't jostle together and smash.

At the campsite the jolly homunculus rolls around on the springy turf, mixes it up with the tent pegs and lawn darts. Chipmunks run over it in the dark, when it's covered with dew.

The children want to take it swimming. Mother doesn't think they should, at first, but Dad says, why not? She finally agrees, but they have to keep a hand on it, so it doesn't float out to sea. She lost a poodle that way once, when she was a child.

It bobs around in the water, its little warty articulations looking like a head-full of grins. The children think they can hear it chuckling.

Dad gets the spare tire out of the trunk and puts it on the picnic table, sets the homunculus inside the ring to dry. Baby tries to feed it part of his egg sandwich, but Mother makes him stop.

Afternoon, they all nap.

Jenny gets up from the stuffy tent about four, and stumbles out looking for cookies. She sees that it's split open, the warty husk peeled away, leaving several brown bobbling wet orbs, transparent, about the size of grapefruit. They're joggling like a jelly, murmuring, small foamy bubbles rise and snap. Jenny thinks again of chuckling.

Now, homunculus is the wrong word. It's just the shell. Jenny picks it up and snaps off all the knobs and warts; it cracks apart like old bark. She tosses the bits into the woods, in ten different directions.

Jenny doesn't have a new word for what's left, but it doesn't matter, it won't be here long. It makes her think of egg yolks cracked into a bowl, before they've been beaten up. They start to slurp and spin, Jenny hitches up her shorts, scratches her back, watches, while they pick up speed, pretty soon the tire's rocking, and then it's down off the table with a bounce, and out along the gravel road, hell bent for leather.

The bits of husk in the woods begin again, of course, but Jenny never knows. They drive back to town that same afternoon, Mother's got her period and just doesn't feel like camping, with a headache.

Unforgettable characters

I wish there was a boarder who'd been an old sea captain; beard, pipe, twinkling eye, who could unscrew his wooden leg. He'd have humped my mother on the kitchen table, winking over at me in my high chair. In Calgary. Landlocked, except for the boisterous Bow.

Or a mistress for my dad, with a glass eye and a freckled bum. Who'd taken him to bars on Saturday nights so he had to deliver his sermons hung over.

Or a gentle octogenarian phantom lover in a motorized wheelchair, lurking in the shrubbery at nursing homes, waiting for afternoon exercise period. Out they'd come, a faltering bevy to take the sun. Bonnets and parasols, trembling chins, voices like paper birds. With a miniature crossbow he'd take out the nurses and attendants with sleep darts, and then have his way with the jumble of shin-bones and canes. Behind the petunia bed, at the corner of the doctors' parking lot.

Or a twin of me, identical, another girl one, so we could stare into each other's faces and do away with mirrors.

Then the sea captain, my dad's mistress with the

freckled bum, the octogenarian phantom lover and the two of me would stay a fortnight at Brighton, walk on the boardwalk, play darts in the pubs at night, and talk and talk, about oysters and Hassidic Jews, the use of the apostrophe, and how the sky turns a deep heartbeat blue above the clear water at the edge of the pack-ice twenty miles by dogsled northwest of Frobisher Bay.

Avant garde

Aroint thee witch, the rump-fed runion cried!

No, wait, that's en garde.

When I was a kid, somebody took me to see Barbara Ann Scott.

No, wait, that's skate guard.

One time we had a boarder from Quebec—this is when we lived in Calgary—who had come west to help change the overhead street wiring to accommodate the larger fire engines the city had purchased. The fire chief was a friend of my dad's, so my dad said the guy could stay with us. He used to come home after a few beers late on Saturday nights and sit and have a cigarette by himself in the dark in the living-room before he went to bed. My mom was afraid he was going to fall asleep and burn the house down.

No, wait, that's Scotch Guard.

My dad had a cousin who was a cabinet-maker for the Canadian Air Force. He made the dashboards and instrument panels for fighter planes. He was very quiet and gentle, and he married a bouncy loquacious woman.

After he retired from the Air Force, the two of them took up ballroom dancing. They won competitions, and became teachers. They travelled all over North America in their camper to go to competitions. One night they invited us, my parents and brother and I, to their house to dance in their rec room. It was windowless, and painstakingly panelled. With all the craft that goes into the dashboard of a fighter bomber. They taught us several steps. Who knows why? I can't now think of any more ludicrous scene than being in our own unfinished basement, en famille, smashing our heads on the furnace pipes, my brother dragging his feet and grumbling.

Anyway, after a couple of invigorating hours of tripping the light fantastic we sat down to sandwiches and lemonade, and the cousin's wife, in a gingerly way, launched into the topic of personal hygiene. Turns out my brother had worked up a sweat and he smelled.

No, wait, that's Right Guard.

Snapshot from the fifties

They're dear, I know, they're a slice of neighbourhood
life, they're from somebody's past, somebody's treasured
past, but I want to shoot them all. It may be the mood I'm
in, it may be because I'm fairly sure I'll be puking by
morning, and my brassiere's too tight, but I want to get a
carbine and topple every one of them out of their pale
winter sunlight backyard misery.

Why am I so hangdog, so vitriolic? Where is this
wretchedness coming from? Is it because the dearness of
these creatures is too strong for me? Is there a danger
that I might care? That I worry that the whole ragtag
bobble tail bunch of them will run into muggers and
rapists when they're scarcely out of their knee socks? So
that I want to shoot them all, now, cleanly and safely,
while they're lined up in somebody's backyard, before
something more horrible gets to them?

Maybe that's not it at all.

Let's look again.

It's not the children, they're ordinary and innocent
enough, it's the green and white plastic awning on the

house behind them. It makes my heart go thunk in terror. What goes *on*, in houses like that? Do grownups loom unwanted into bedrooms? Is the bath water too hot? Does the cat get trapped behind the furnace and strangle? On Sunday afternoons do they look at slides of the Holy Land until they shriek and scream with boredom and gnaw each other's knuckles, are their goddamn sleeves at such a stylishly awkward length that their arms hang out like broomsticks, do they eat tomato aspic and pickled beets, oh WHAT depraved maniacal under-god ever invented those green and white plastic awnings?

Those simple, neat, maintenance-free, boring awnings.

Work thoughts

It's quiet. A couple of them, at the table behind me, are looking into their microscopes. I'm sitting at my microfilm camera, flipping 'em through, flipping 'em through. My piano-trained fingers hover over the keypad. Name, date, EXPOSE; name, date, EXPOSE. The rhythm settles, and my mind starts to travel.

Why go to Hell when you can go to Toronto? That's what my father said when he was a kid.

The TH&B (Toronto, Hamilton and Buffalo) was To Hell and Back.

My mother had a friend in college called Helen Augusta Wind. Get it? Hell, and a gust of wind.

When they wanted to say Hell, when my father was a kid, and anybody's parents were around, they said Dundas.

Go to Hell was Go to Grass.

Cow manure was kack-kack.

Having a shit was doin' tacks.

It was a big joke when my dad got us lost in Hamilton, in a blizzard, him having been born there and all.

My mother had another friend, in her dormitory,

who'd go out in the dark in her roadster after a rain and pop frogs on the highway.

Quick Henry, the Flit! That's something they said a lot. It was from a bug-spray ad.

They played a game, my father and his friends, called Mama! Mama! The kettle's boiling over! The person playing the part of Mama would then say, Take a spoon and stir it. End of game. Then they picked someone else to be Mama.

Another of my mother's college friends, her roommate, was from Chile. When she went back, after four years, she wouldn't give anyone her address, because it was too dangerous to receive foreign mail. My mother has since had her die a thousand deaths.

When my dad was a kid, he and his friends skated out to the Burlington Bridge. Not that there was one. They skated out to the gap the Burlington Bridge now spans. Then they turned around, and opened their coats, and let the wind drive them back right across Hamilton harbour (where Lady Simcoe saw giant turtles swimming a hundred-and-fifteen years earlier).

My girlfriend's brother had a raft he built and kept hidden in the Dundas marsh. His mother never knew about it. Saturdays they floated all over the marsh. The turtles were still there, then. Probably the same ones. By now they'll have choked to death on Stelco effluent.

Toronto is hell. War is hell. War is not pretty. Hamilton

is a blue-collar town, Boris Brott notwithstanding.

I stop working, stretch my arms, and tell them that once Boris Brott's mother was in hospital, down the hall from an expert whistler, and she convinced her husband, Alexander Brott, to hire the whistler to whistle a concerto with the Montreal Symphony.

Then I go back to it: name, date, EXPOSE.

Five minutes later, one woman looks up from her microscope and says, 'Oh, look here, this poor bugger's going to have to have his leg cut off.'

Kincardine

I can't open it. I can't even look right at it and feel bad.
I can't feel anything. The lake's done curving, done its
Grand Bend, and settled down to head north for a while
into Kincardine. A small gully, it's winter for God's sake,
and this little bundle of bunched baby lay out there with
the wet leaves and dogshit and he died.

People lie to their kids all the time. Continually. Inten-
tionally and unintentionally.

'Don't …' and the kid does.

'If you stand on that you'll fall …' and the kid
doesn't fall.

'If you're not good Santa Claus won't come …' and the
kid's a shit and Santa comes anyway.

Words mean nothing.

So, okay. A kid can survive that, slide through the
school system, even if he drops out and goes into the
streets and mugs old ladies he's still got body and soul
together. Doesn't need words. He can still eat and shit and
fornicate, even with nowhere solid to put his feet down.

But dying before he can even walk, out there with the

wet leaves and the dogshit, that's something else again.

Dying means all the breath goes out for the last time and never comes in again. Dead battery.

What'd she do, strangle it, drop it, belt it one because she couldn't stand the way the light came through her filthy apartment window on just too much daytime TV?

Sometimes I want to squeeze my cats so hard they squirt. I've shovelled a few off the road. Buried them, in the middle of the swarming flies.

Once I hit a mouse with a two-by-four.

My father died, dear heaven, we all know my father died.

It's how their mouths fold around a spoon of applesauce, that I wouldn't want stopped. They're so small. Compact.

When your mother doesn't love you, whole gaping subterranean chutes open up and the entire world, aspen leaves and loons and Mozart, wet rain on the highway, the D minor scale, four octaves, hands together, the whole world disappears like hot party vomit into a smoking snowbank. Melting, melting, finding no bottom, it all disappears and there's nothing left to stand on; might as well lie with the other refuse in a gully, the McDonald's bags, the condoms, the lost golf balls, wet leaves and dogshit.

The dream

The dream began with her little naked bum. I had it cradled in my hand, and then I became aware that I was holding the entire child. She was lost, but in no apparent distress. This much was clear: I had a lost naked child.

But where was I? Will this bloody dream not open up? Will you open up this bloody dream, I have a lost naked child here. Then it clears. The *mise en scène*.

Shit. It's Simpsons. It's one of the Simpsons Christmas nightmares, six weeks early. There's the back staircase, there's the freight elevator, there's the high window with the pebbled glass, letting in the grey-green light, how many *times* have I been set to dream through this store, can I never get it right and have done with it?

Ladies' dresses, the nasty saleswoman in her girdle, why send me here with this defenceless child? So many times before: I've been locked in, locked out, I've fallen down the stairs, I've wet my pants on the broadloom, I've climbed a ladder to smash at the pebbled glass with a sixty dollar stiletto heel, I've shoplifted and got caught, I've shoplifted and got away, I've eaten floss candy in

ladies' outerwear and got it gummed into the fur coats,
I've suffocated with my head stuck into the tartan kilts.

The elevator's let loose, the elevator's jammed, the
lights have gone out, a big-nosed clown has slid his fingers into my underpants, I've had a bathing-suit stuck on
my head in the fitting room, choking on latex.

And now they send me here with a small naked
girlchild in my arms, who's lost her mother. She doesn't
know her name. She only knows the town where she
lives. I have to find her mother, I have to grit my teeth and
focus on finding her mother, or the dream will flip us outside and I'll have to return her to the nursery school
where the cookies are poisoned.

The dream will rip her out of my arms and force her
into that death-trap nursery school.

I phone the Chamber of Commerce in the town where
she lives. It's Saturday. They closed at noon, everybody's
gone but the janitor. He knows the lunch bar where the
boss will be having a sandwich. He'll try to call him. He'll
get back to me. The child squirms. The store closes down
around us and goes black.

Mary and Ann

The woman must have a forearm of iron. She's balancing, on one hand, a full-blown child in the throes of religious ecstasy. Holding it as easily as if it were a pound of butter, or a walnut. The child, all unaware of its precarious perch, sitting there like a jolly marmot in some kind of nightgown affair, grins up at the sky.

The woman's own gown, shit-brown, drapes to the floor. No breeze disturbs its plaster folds. The toes of her two sensibly tailored boots poke out below the hem.

It's a Mother and Child, but not the ones we've grown accustomed to seeing, from cathedrals to dashboards. No, it's the next generation back. The *grand*mother of Himself, the Paschal Lamb, the Dove, our Lord and Saviour whether we want Him or not. And His mother, as a child. A grinning marmot child, making her first electric contact with the lord of the skies who will eventually, in the fullness of time, come ripping down and impregnate her. Trying to get a taste of carnality into his airy-fairy ineffable life. A jolt or two. A couple of spikes through the wrist. A little dash of vinegar on the tongue.

Just to see what it's like. Here, stick these metal tweezers into that open wall socket. These fucking incorporeal angels, you can shove your hand right through them.

So anyway here's the grandmother, with this perfectly usable daughter, a little old in the face, maybe, but comely enough, with a certain capacity for merriment. And instead of leaving well enough alone, the woman shows the girl how to part the clouds, part her legs, draw down upon herself forces better left alone, draw down upon all of us these hundreds of years of agony, guilt, remorse, torture, white gloves, patent leather shoes, Christmas shopping; a general swamp of mass-culture self-abnegation.

Her head is bent in the general direction of the moonstruck child, but her gaze goes past her, fixed on the lower middle distance. One hand raised in an attitude of instruction, a gesture of admonition, the eternal sell-out of daughters by their mothers. (Think about it, He's a God! We'll all get to move in with Him maybe, or at the very least get this place air-conditioned.)

All this is from the front. What we might see when passing a niche in a hallway, or gazing up past an altar. But we have the incredible good fortune to have this specimen free-standing on our kitchen floor. Where we can see the most private of parts, the grandmother's back. Straight, quiet, desperate, this silent back tells of the misery she herself has suffered, the iron will that has focused her bitter venom onto this petted girlchild prize, the daughter she's grooming to bear the Ultimate Victim, the Sponge, the Tonsil, destined to suck up the sins of the world.

Litany

What do you want, the old crabbed auntie says,
Which of my things do you especially treasure?
What do you want of mine to remember me by
when I'm gone?

Back at the beginning, they said nothing.
Nothing, they said politely, don't talk of dying.
That was enough, for then. She was able to take that
small response into the gaping maw of her heart, embroi-
der it, elaborate on it. She decided that for them to imagine her death was too painful. They must really love her.

They must really love her! She took this crumb and
scuttled back with it to her fetid den. Licked it, gnawed
at it, toyed with it, preened.

Finally it was all gone.

Into the quaking emptiness she said, what if they
don't love me?

What do you want, the auntie says,
Which of my things do you especially treasure?
What do you want of mine to remember me by

when I'm gone?

Nothing, they said. We'll have our memories. We want nothing.

This wasn't good enough. She'd used it all up.

Don't you like any of my things? They're all so precious to me. Each one represents a dear memory. Does my life mean nothing to you?

Of course it does, they said. We don't spurn your things. We *like* your things. We just don't want to entertain the idea of choosing one.

Back she scuttled. They *like* my things. They like my *things!* They like the way I have them so tastefully displayed! They *like* me. They *love* me!

Until it was all used up, too.

Out she came, blinking through her tears.

What do you want?
Which of my things do you especially treasure?
What do you want of mine to remember me by
when I'm gone?

I'm going to sort things, she said, slyly. Give things away to the poor.

Trapped, they declared themselves.

We want the moccasins. The tiny doll moccasins, so meticulously stitched and beaded. The moccasins that sat, untouchable, in the glassed-in cabinet when we were children.

They did it. Chose something. Declared themselves.
Silence from her cave.

I've sent the tiny moccasins to the museum. You didn't
want them, did you?

They're silent. They don't say, yes, we did. It's beyond
that. They've been cornered, enticed, trapped, sandbagged.
She can't stand the silence.

What do you want?
Which of my things do you especially treasure?
What do you want of mine to remember me by
when I'm gone?

They took a deep breath.

We want the plastic fruit, that you keep in a carton in
the attic. The faded banana, the orange, and the cluster of
bright blue grapes. Laced together with plastic-coated
wire. That we bought for you for a quarter; money we'd
saved, at a time when our allowance was only a dime. We
saw the plastic fruit, and imagined how you would love it.
We ran to your house with it, breathless; we couldn't wait
until you took it out of its wrapping.

You hated it. You told us you hated it. You laughed, and
said whatever possessed you to purchase such a thing.

That's what we want. We want that plastic fruit, gar-
ishly painted, and we want its bitter memory. We want
that dark memory to sit on our mantel, forever.

That's what we want.

Domestic bliss

Superman has flown into somebody's backyard for a swim. Fresh from the pool, dripping, he's still got his outfit on; his tights are wrinkling around his ankles. He picks up a towel from one of the plastic deck chairs. It's a Batman towel.

Fuck, says Superman, and throws it in the pool.

He waves his arms to get dry. Steps into his superboots. They slurp and squlch as he walks around the deck.

He finds a half-opened pack of cigarettes on one of the round white plastic tables. They're Popeye cigarettes.

Fuck, says Superman, and throws them in the pool.

He keeps walking. Squlch, squlch, squlch, in his superboots. There's a watch on the diving board. Somebody's left it there to keep it dry, and then forgotten about it. It's rained on it, and there's condensation inside the crystal. He can't tell what time it is. He gets a swizzle stick somebody's left in an ashtray, and pries off the cloudy crystal. It's a Wonder Woman watch.

Fuck, says Superman, and throws it in the pool.

Squlch, squlch, squlch.

He's wet, there's no smokes, and he doesn't know what time it is.

Where the fuck is everybody? he shouts.

Three Jehovah's Witnesses who have been lurking in the lane see this as their big chance. They open the garden gate and come running in.

Good afternoon, Sir, lovely afternoon isn't it, are you familiar with the publications *Watchtower* and *Awake?*

Superman stops and looks at them.

Who puts them out? he says. *Watchtower* and *Awake?*

God, they say.

Fuck, says Superman, and throws them in the pool. All three of them. One after the other.

Plip, plip, plop. The three Jehovah's Witnesses go flopping into the pool, briefcases and all. Their ties float up around their ears.

Just then the lady of the house comes home with the groceries. Superman hears her coming.

Fuck, he says, and flies away.

She staggers into the house with bags and bags of groceries, and drops them on the kitchen floor and goes out on the deck to have a cigarette.

In the pool are the Batman towel, the Popeye cigarettes, the broken Wonder Woman watch and three flailing Jehovah's Witnesses. Their briefcases have come open, and the ink from their *Watchtowers* and *Awakes* is discolouring the water.

Fuck, says the housewife and jumps into the pool. She swims around and collects everything and throws it all up onto the apron. She leaves the Jehovah's Witnesses to last.

Just then the man of the house comes home from work. He puts his attaché case, his bowling ball and his empty Tim Horton plastic coffee mug down in the kitchen and goes out on the deck for a cigarette.

In the pool are his wife, with all her clothes on, crying, and three half-drowned Jehovah's Witnesses.

Fuck, says the man of the house. He goes back in and gets his bowling ball, carries it up onto the diving board, and drops it into the pool. The tidal wave floats the three religious near-corpses up onto the apron. His wife, crying and sputtering, sinks to the bottom of the pool. The bowling ball rolls onto her foot.

Just then the kids of the house come home from Brownies, hockey, ballet and 4-H. They put down their beanie, skates, toe shoes and twin baby calves in the kitchen and go out on the deck to sneak a cigarette.

In the deep end of the pool is their mother, pinned to the bottom by a bowling ball. On the diving board is their dad, looking distraught. He still has his suit jacket on. On the apron there's a whole bunch of garbage and three dead Jehovah's Witnesses.

Fuck, the kids say. Too bad Superman's not here.

Introspection

Okay, so suppose one day's worth of events does go into one brain cell, I guess I can give you that, let's adopt it for a working model, but we have to account for overlap, for the fact that a quick sudden sight of a kid pulling a pike out of the water under a railway trestle can activate a good half-dozen memories, all unlooked for, suddenly accessed from their own day's-worth brain cells, where they were quietly tucked dozing away in a row in the archival fridge. And does *this* day's brain cell include all of that? Or is there a night-staff who straighten out the files while we sleep, put the grumbling brain cells of the previous days who were so rudely called upon to cough up their memories back in order? And are they then untouched, the same as they were? Or if, on some idle ramble, we're rummaging through that older day, will we not shoot suddenly forward to today's kid, today's pike and trestle, and then not splatter laterally, headlong, into all those other glistening singing images?

Last memory one

The ceiling was blue. It went up to a dome with tiny windows around its base, so that light came in onto the painted plaster. Or not, depending on the day. Or maybe the obscurity was in my mind. As the days passed, it seemed less important.

Most of my waking thoughts were of the white bird. It flew around the dome, or perched on a window ledge, preened, slept, let droppings carelessly plummet through the still air. None of them ever reached me, although I do remember a shadowy figure wiping my face. But that could have been anything—sweat from a fever, spilled apple juice, tears.

Not only my waking thoughts. I dreamed of the bird as well. In dreams it was larger, and it flew outside the dome, across a moor or marshland, through a thin sifting of mist. Sometimes I watched, sometimes I went with it, flying along beside, sometimes I *was* it, peering down from my dark round marble bird eyes.

Only occasionally could I locate myself there, specifically there, lying on the bed, looking at the blue curve of the ceiling, knowing my toes were somewhere off a body-length away, pointing up. I was having just such a moment of clarity, remembering the colour and texture of the telegram from overseas at the end of the war, and just exactly how my heart had thudded, when the dome suddenly faded, the bird and I were surrounded in mist, and here we are now, together, still flying.

from the *Dragonfly Notebook*

Now this is a kitchen where it's safe to spill sugar. That's something, anyway. The diabetic kid from the day care won't lick it up. The killer ants won't swarm out of the drains, and in their enthusiasm pick the baby clean.

No, spill all the sugar you want, and then just brush it up with a damp J Cloth.

Nor is there any problem with letting these walnut shells pile up on the violin part for Bartok's Roumanian Dances. Nor any real difficulty with the fact that of the seven I've opened, four have been withered. No sun-up firing squads out on the Walnut Collectives. I know when to keep my mouth shut. No skulls under shovels, toy or otherwise.

So whaddya mean, you wanna get off?

Take the train or get outa the kitchen.

True enough, some nights there's vomit, and killer bees. But usually there's the smell of pies in the oven, the kettle bubbles happily, the well-named cats sleepily suck at themselves over the heat register while the wind plays merrily in the eaves.

Don't you want to see what happens? Will we end up in the Elysian Fields, or under the ice in some dark tree-fringed lake?

Aren't you even a little bit curious about the names of the cats?

No?

So leave.

Shut the door.

Real life

An adolescent girl sits on a plaid blanket before the camp-fire, leaning back against a log. She's in a ring of glowing singing faces. She has crushes on her female cabin-group leader, her male canoe-trip leader, Mozart, and God. *Someone's dying, Lord*, she sings, *kum ba ya*. Sparks burst above the flames and disappear into the black sky.

Loudspeaker in the hospital corridor: Code seven. Four northwest.

The blood gas machine has calibrated, it's ready to go. They wait for the running footsteps. Faint at first, coming through the door at the end of the hall, then sneakers thudding up closer. A panting nurse thrusts the blood sample in at the window, fixes a strand of hair, while they process it and write the results on the requisition. They hand it back to her and off she goes at a trot, her footsteps become fainter and disappear through the door.

Someone's dying, Lord, on four northwest.

Epaulets

How many years have I been going *on* about epaulets, I'm so sick of it now, so sick of the person that needs to say interesting things about epaulets.

When the topic was young and fresh, when I was young and fresh, when it was a new idea, it was as close as I ever got to an epiphany. I'll explain it again, maybe for the last time.

American soldiers have epaulets on their uniforms, and Russian soldiers have epaulets on their uniforms, but they're enemies. How can people, in any military encounter, stand there and try to blast each other's heads off when they're wearing the same silly little flaps of cloth on their shoulders? If they can agree on what is appropriate to wear when they kill each other, why can't they agree on whatever it is they're trying to kill each other *about?*

Well, there it is. It comes from the era when I was a bit of a darling for my interesting mind. I'd toss back a straight scotch at a party, and launch into epaulets. Always trying to recapture the heightened state, the brilliant quality of light, the cosmic certainty that was there when I first thought of it.

It was like trying to wheedle back a lost lover, or the attention of a toddler. Once I remember sitting on the carpet under someone's grand piano, after several more than one scotch, crying quietly, muttering, drunkenly, *epaulet*, pleading with the gods of vision gods of grace to give me back that straight belt of octane.

But I'm done with that now. Epaulets can lie about on my closet floor like some disused faintly gynecological cast-off. A placenta, say, or tripe. Skateboard with the trucks off. An old sweater three sizes too big and the wrong colour.

Piss off, epaulets. Who needs you?

Essential

It's the last thing to go, or what you'd throw to safety first in a fire.

The Ground Bass. Pachelbel's Canon. Or Donald Sutherland's state of mind, sitting in his garage, realizing his love for Mary Tyler Moore had just run out.

I never knew, when I was younger, if fundament means tail-bone, or excreted material. I still don't.

Tampax, I suppose. And the theatre tickets. Anything else, you can do without or buy when you get there.

Heart pills.

Underwear.

Dentures.

A wet sheet and a flowing sea and a wind that follows fast.

Princess Margaret Rose said, on Desert Island Discs, that she would choose Tennessee Ernie Ford singing 'Sixteen Ton.'

and Non-essential?

Kissing Mick Jagger is one thing I can do without.

I don't need toothpicks, I use my hair.

Doors

Jim Morrison was Charlie's hero. Charlie the army brat, middle kid of seven, Mensa member, hop-head, blustery foul-mouthed blowhard Charlie.

I'd be working away, cutting out little pictures of cars and trucks, sticking them onto the flats, six to a page. Top two facing in, second two out, the little sticky strips of type, fresh out of the aromatic waxer, along the bottom of each picture.

> 1964 MGB, silver, convertible, standard, looks good, runs good. Georgia car, no rust, no bondo. No tire-kickers. Married, must sell, little woman can't handle stick.

Brian, running in and out, making a projected page count. Lance, the aesthete, heaving great melodramatic sighs, his moustache twitching. Debbie muttering quiet baby-talk to the cars as she worked: 'There you go, little Datsun!'

Charlie stood behind us all, slamming contact sheets in and out of the developer, objecting to some woman on the radio: 'Shut that wailing slut up, I can't concentrate.'

Lance, in effusive disgust, leaping up to the radio, 'All *right*, Charlie,' turning it down with a flourish.

Into the silence I'd absent-mindedly hum a bit of Doors and Charlie would take off with it, sing us the whole song, then the whole album, say, 'He's not really dead, ya know, it was all an elaborate plot.'

'Well, fuck a duck,' said Brian. Or, sometimes, 'Holy ducks on toast.'

Charlie had a friend who cooked at a Mexican restaurant. She brought him lunch every couple of weeks. Blue was the only flavour Chiclets he would chew. He came off his motorcycle once and was dragged down Wellington street half a block, the bike on top of him, his pant cuff hooked over a lady's bumper. Came in scraped head to foot. Took off his shirt and socks, to show us the scabs. I almost had him convinced to take off his pants, until fastidious Lance objected.

'S'matter, Lance,' Charlie said, 'afraid to look at some real meat?'

Lunch times, Charlie and I would sometimes be the only ones still working. A two-page layout for a dealer, whacking 'em down. He'd talk to me then, quietly, the Real Charlie. Tell me about his mom, and his childhood. I told him that my kid had made a cheesecake one night, for me to eat when I got home from work. He almost cried. 'Sounds like a good kid,' he said. If Lance had been in the room, Charlie'd have had to say, 'What is your kid, a fucking faggot?'

The nose

Yesterday my nose got itchy. I scratched it. It didn't help. I buried it in a mound of fresh-chopped onions. It didn't help. I phoned my mother. *She* said, it means you're going to kiss a fool. I've tried that, I said, it didn't work out. She had nothing else to offer. I phoned my spiritual advisor. He said I should go out to a graveyard at midnight and ram my nose up a cat's ass. I decided to switch churches.

I got a sheet of industrial-grade sandpaper and rubbed my nose with that. It got very shiny, and then started to bleed. The neighbour's kid said I should go to the hospital. Which one? I said. I've withdrawn from one Catholic institution already today. The neighbour's kid is only two. He didn't know what I was talking about. He got on his tricycle and rode around in circles pretending to be an ambulance while my nose dripped blood onto his driveway. Wee ooo Wee ooo, he said. His mother came out of the house to hit him, and saw me standing there, with blood all over my shoes. She also said I should go to the hospital. A more informed opinion.

The lights in Emergency were very bright. They

wrapped a towel around my face and gave me a clipboard with a questionnaire on it. What is the chief end of man, it said. I wrote: THE NOSE.

The Residents were puzzled. The Doctors were puzzled. The Specialists were puzzled. They called in the two volunteer crones who sell chocolate bars in the gift shop.

Ladies, said the medical personnel in chorus, what shall we do with this woman's nose?

Cut it off, cut it off, they cackled. Banging each other over the blue rinse hairdos with Mr. Goodbars.

When I woke up, they were studying the slides of the cross-sectional slices they'd taken of my nose after it was amputated. One after the other. Slide upon slide, with slice upon slice of my nose, pared to a uniform unicellular thickness.

It still itched. The slides rattled in their metal case. The itch was multiplied a hundredfold. Each slide itched with the intensity of the former total nose. Microscopic itch-balls were escaping into the air. Soon all the Doctors and Nurses and Scrub-persons and Volunteers were clawing at each other's starched uniforms. They began to murmur and then to shriek and scream.

I was unmoved by it all. I lay on my back, staring into the mirror beside the operating table, studying the black hole in the centre of my face. Itchless and alone. At peace.

A small child came down from Paediatrics to see what all the racket was. He brought his hamster. Hey lady, he said, when he spotted the hole, can Midge get in there? Sure, I said. Why not.

So Midge got in there, and built a nest, and she doesn't itch like the old nose used to. Sometimes she keeps me awake at night, running on her little wheel. But I don't mind. I hum little songs to the rhythm of the wheel until she's tired, and then we both fall asleep.

Foreplay

'I'll be there in a jiffy, I just have to wash my hands, just a jiffy, while I close the curtains, wait! The stereo's about run down, I'll stack on some more records, you sure you're not hungry? Oh God, the cat! I have to put *her* out or she'll jump on the sofa, you going to be warm enough, shall I build a fire?'

She lay flat on her back. Naked. Counting, slowly, in French, by fives, wiggling her toes up, and then down, at each count, watching them wiggle, focusing first on her toes, then on the wallpaper behind them, then on her toes, thinking about how much trouble this would be, this changing focus, if you were trying to do it in a movie, thinking how much easier it was just to force her eyes to do it.

He rushed past, between her feet and the wallpaper, in his tuxedo shirt, his underwear, his socks and garters, with a bowl of chips. Set them on the coffee table beside her.

'Sorry. I won't be a moment. Salt and vinegar okay? I'm just putting them here now so we won't have to get up afterwards. Do you think the music's too loud?'

She continued to count. Wondered how many hyphens there were in trois cent soixante-cinq. Wiggled her toes.

He sat down on the coffee table, facing her, undid his garters, peeled off his socks, folded them. Jumped up.

'Just a jiffy! Might as well put these in the laundry hamper right now. Oh Christ! I don't know if I have any condoms. Oh shit. That bastard took my last one with him to Bracebridge! Fuck!'

He slammed the bathroom cabinet.

'Back in a jiff! I'll just nip down to the corner. Eat some chips!' He grabbed his coat and stepped barefoot into his boots. The door slammed.

Quatre cent quinze.

She reached down on the floor beside her, picked up her purse, balanced it on her naked belly while she rummaged inside. Found a package of condoms. Took one out. Put the rest back in the purse, the purse back on the floor. Stretched it out, like an elastic band, then blew it up like a balloon, tied a knot at the end, and tossed it lightly up towards the ceiling. Milky-white, it looked like a bladder. It floated back down to her, and she bounced it on her fingertips. Pong, float. Pong, float.

When she heard his key in the lock she caught it, broke it with the sharp corner of the channel-changer, and stuffed it down behind the sofa cushion.

Cinq cent quatre-vingt-cinq.

The missing wife

The scenario, here, tawdry but full of detail, the murky downtown backstreet bar, four o'clock on a February Wednesday, the pimp, the whore, two cops, a bartender and the hero, all mixing it up with ripped shirts, chairs and the sound of sirens. The hero with anchor tattoos on his forearms.

But what suburban scene houses the hero's wife? What sheets does he crawl between, anchored forearms and all? She is, after all, the formal cause of this imbroglio, absent in body, but present in the passion, the anger, the flying spit that passes among this handful of overwrought people.

Is she at a stove, putting on the vegetables, watching the leaden sky turn to black, caught for a moment in contemplation of the roller-skate key on the window ledge? Absent from herself, feeling the pull, perhaps, of the violent interchange downtown in the bar, the shadow of it passing causing her to stop, water dripping from her ladle onto the stove.

She hears the TV from the living-room, they'll be out

here soon, bugging her, wanting their supper, the baby's already starting to fuss, her attention not yet gripped by the flickering images. She imagines the faces of the older two, slack and absorbed, only the pupils of their eyes moving; rouses herself, goes to the living-room door to look, sees that she was right, and then watches as both small faces break into grins. The hero has won. None of the children notices her watching them.

And downtown, there's the paddywagon, she hasn't received the call yet to tell her he won't be home. His torn flannel shirt silently sucks water out of the spittoon in the darkened corner.

Flight

She's on the train, in the dining car, smoking, looking at the flushed-out mid-March wood lots. It's the children, of course, that cause the welling sadness. It's always the children.

This morning, at the beginning, to get up, to get organized, to get out, there had been the double energy of adrenalin and resolve. Culminating in the station, when she suddenly shed the roles; bought cigarettes and a magazine at the kiosk. She felt the past draining away like a miscarriage or the flushing of a toilet as the train accelerated through the suburbs, and then, in her anonymity among the other passengers, the high octane jolt of a thousand possibilities.

She decided to make her first free act a walk to the dining car, a cup of coffee.

It was mid-afternoon, between meals, the tables cleared but not set again. The waiter was sitting at the end of the car in his shirt sleeves, talking to the cook in black talk, so paced and exotic as to sound unlike English at all. He brought her coffee, smiled, his waiter's suaveté taken off with his jacket. The man here, mid-afternoon, whose job is waitering, not the Waiter Himself she might have seen an hour earlier. He went back to sit with the cook. Now she's halfway through the pack of cigarettes, the coffee cup's empty, a beige ring from the wet spoon has spread into the tablecloth, there are crumbs left from a stranger's luncheon roll, a scrunched up napkin, a smear of lipstick. And she sits, watching the clumps of aspen appear, present themselves, recede, stringy-looking trees slanting out of mud and patches of punky snow.

And she thinks, not directly about the children; that full frontal pain will come later, probably tonight when she climbs, shivering, into her hotel bed. But obliquely. Tangentially. She thinks adjacent to the children, about the square of sunlight that's beginning to appear these spring days on the hardwood floor outside the baby's room. She smells pablum and spit-up, the vague pervasive stench of soaking diapers, ammonia. The smells well up in her mind along with the patch of sunlight without her even realizing it.

The sunlight moves across the floor, she tears her mind away at the last moment, before the toddler calls out, is it time to get up yet, tears it frantically, like the tearing of a scab. She lights another cigarette, forces herself, plunges her mind screaming into boiling water, thinks about sitting for him, shivering, day after day in the cold studio. While he works meticulously, absorbed, conscious of her only as shape, as angled plane, the grey light spilling onto his canvas. She thinks of his filthy sweater, his ashtray, the smell of his unshowered body; and the hatred comes back with a rush, beating like hot blood, flushes out the image of the waking children and their lustrous sleepy mouths.

The garden

He's about to be seven. It's tomorrow. Zero days, not counting today. After one more sleep.

It's closer than it's ever been, he's been waiting actively for two months now, marking off the calendar on his bedroom wall with a red crayon.

But the closer he gets, the slower everything moves. Now, for instance, he's in his room for his afternoon quiet time. He's too old to call it a nap any more. Next fall he won't *have* any quiet time, because he'll be in school all day.

He can do anything he likes; he just has to stay in there. This seems like the longest quiet time he's ever had. He's lying on his bed, crosswise, on his stomach, with his forehead against the window pane. Looking down into the garden. He knows how hot it is; he was out there this morning. The lace edges on the tablecloth hang down, down, weighted. There's a bowl of flowers on the table. One petal from a rose falls as he watches. Rocks gently, settles. He wants to run out and grab it, stick it back onto the plant. A petal about to fall is better than one that's finally fallen.

Susan is downstairs vacuuming. The lace on the table-cloth reminds him of the lace on her apron. What she always wears. A black dress and a white apron. Sunday nights, when his parents are out, Susan lets him come into her room and watch 'Star Trek' on her television, while she irons her black uniforms. She hangs them up one by one on the door sill. Black puppet Susans. He watches them accumulate. Susan and shadow Susans.

Both 'Star Treks'. The old one and then the new one. Two hours. Susan has seen all the old ones before. If she's in a bad mood she tells him what's going to happen next.

Another crimson petal has fallen. He hasn't seen it drop. It's there, beside the first one. He can't stand it. He wants them back up where they belong.

Suddenly he springs from the bed, races downstairs, out the back door—Susan is in the living-room—and into the garden. Quiet time isn't over, on the clock, but he can't stand it. He takes the two petals, one in each hand, and sets them up among the blossoms in the bowl. They rest there, like floating feathers, but the motion causes others to fall. He counts them. Five. He picks them up, one by one, balances them on top. More fall.

He takes the big bunch of flowers out of the bowl, his two hands grabbing around the thorny stems, and shakes them. He can hear himself making a soft, high-pitched moony sound; his ears feel too full, like he's under water. Shakes them, crimson all over the white, he clutches the cloth corner in one hand, runs with it, swoops it off the table, the bowl falls and breaks, he dives under the hedge, into the cool green dapple earth brown silence and lies, stomach down, face in the dirt, sobbing.

Rachel can't get the twins to stop fighting

Ellie's slumped in the back of the station-wagon. The very farthest back she can get. In fact, she's tugged the spare tire out of the wheel well, and crowded a great deal of her small self down into the space. She's looking out the back window. Watching everything woosh past, and then grow tiny and disappear.

She's muttering.

'Puke. He's a puke. He's a goddamn puke.'

Very quiet muttering, because if her mother ever heard her say goddamn she'd really be in for it.

It's Jim's turn to sit in front, he's up there beside Rachel, chattering away, Ellie knows he's chattering in that particularly engaging way to get her goat. There's no one she knows better than she knows her brother.

'Goddamn puke.'

'Did you say something, Ellie?'

Ellie can hear the pleading in Rachel's voice. She's something of an expert on voices. She wishes her mother wouldn't plead. There's something wrong with it—it makes her feel faintly sick to her stomach.

She doesn't answer. Instead, she begins to develop the idea of being sick. Right here, right now, over her knees and into the wheel well. That would serve her right. Serve them both right. They'd have to find a washroom, stop, clean up the car, get a drink of water, she'd get to sit in the front, they wouldn't have to go to the stupid zoo. The more she thinks about it, the better it sounds.

'Ellie, did you *hear* me? I'm asking you a question.' Ellie freezes, mid-dream, becomes invisible, the long-tailed cone of road still disappearing out behind.

Jim says, 'She's just being a suck.'

That snaps it.

'You're a *puke*,' she screams.

'Suck!'

'Puke!'

'Suck!'

'Goddamn puke!'

Slam on the brakes. Ellie's head smashes against the back of the seat behind her.

She's said it. Goddamn. Jim's too astonished to go on fighting.

The three of them sit there. This is more than a tiresome game; some threshold has been crossed. When Ellie finally looks up towards the front of the car, she sees Jim, in profile, his eye round with shock. In the rear-view mirror, Rachel's eyes are beginning to fill with tears.

Liver ∂acrilege

The path runs narrowly down a cobbled walkway, littered with slugs, bean slugs, curdled slugs, slugs hanging on fern leaves, grappling with spiders, succubus slugs on sodden trunks, thick as a liver, wet with dew. Deeper still, cobbled still, below these dank monastic walls, through to the heart of it, vacuoles, systoles, diastoles, diatonic scales from the liver-wet throats of the monks, semen-smeared soutanes, egg on the collars. The slugs congregate, heap up, sweat to the shrunken breviaries, throats in unison, monk throats, slug throats, Brother Wendell's bent finger pokes along the crooked page.

Brother Hilary slips from the chancel, picks up a basket at the scullery door, out into the fig banked dewy morning. He stands silent in the kitchen garden, marvelling at the writhing slugs, heaped in ecstasy sucking the mournful song from the monk-throats. Stands, stares, then scuttles down the path, long red sausage-fingers into the slugpile, heaping dripping coiling handfuls into the basket, harvest of roiling mucus and slime. He staggers back, heaping basket, across the kitchen garden, in through the scullery, monk-throats singing, all morning, every morning, mornings of endless timeless slug slime, shuffles to the cauldron, over the fireplace, swings it out, basket balanced on his hip, then tipped, edged up over the boiling water. Hand up to elbow in slug-wet, pulling them out, out of the basket, into the bath, scum froth slug juice boils on the water top. He swings the cauldron back over the fire, the houinhouinhouin of vaporous slug-souls, coiling, dying.

Brother Wendell's bent finger stops over the manuscript, in a monkish breath-gap, morning air dew-laden breath-gap. Finger-stopping slug-whine, then slime gurgle monk song on again, slug bodies curl, coil, drop to the cauldron bottom. Brother Hilary skims the slime-froth with a giant wooden paddle, brings it to his lips, tongue pink liver-tongue dabbles in the slime foam, adds a bayleaf, three dried peppercorns. Monks in the chancel, singing for their supper.

The head

It was getting pretty tense, with her carping at him all the time, she never knows when to stop, and finally Harold just lost his head.

Well, I can tell you that set her back. She didn't want to admit it was missing, at first, just went on talking about the flower show, and the crowds on the buses, but eventually the sight of his headless body sitting there in the wicker chair in front of the window, its legs crossed, drumming its fingers on the end table, made even her stop.

For the first time in *my* living memory, anyway, she didn't know what to say. She looked around sort of helplessly, but nobody was watching. God knows Harold couldn't see her, his eyes had gone with the head, and Reginald and Chester and the rest of us just stared down at her from our ornate frames. I remember she used to get that same peevish frustrated look when she was a little girl throwing a tantrum and no one would pay attention. Her father the Duke, rest his soul and pass the catsup, insisted that tantrums be ignored. He was a great hand with horses.

When she couldn't collect an audience, when she finally realized that she was Truly Alone, she began to look at Harold curiously. More particularly at the stump that throbbed quietly inside the ring of his shirt collar. It seemed like a clean separation, no gore, no slime, as if Harold's head had been one of those plastic pop-off beads the grandchildren sometimes cart in here to play with.

He couldn't hear, of course, or taste, see or smell, but his fingers still drummed, his foot in its leather slipper still bounced gently up and down.

When she'd had a good look at the socket, she began to glance furtively around for the whereabouts of the head. Standing there, at first, rotating slightly, looking with her eyes. Then she began to move around, stoop, look under chairs and sofas, down behind the piano.

Harold drumming the while, swinging his foot, no urgency from *his* quarter for his missing top seventh.

She passed the bell-rope, but she didn't want to ring. She wanted to find the head, and restore it, and go on as usual, before anyone else came in. So she kept on looking.

Harold's head, meanwhile, carrying most of the features by which we would, on an ordinary day, identify Harold, was rolling down the road like the Gingerbread Boy. Even he remarked on the similarity. *Run, run, as fast as you can*, he muttered to himself. He turned into a lane that led to a hayfield, and rolled right to the centre of it. Then he stopped, turned, and looked back at the road.

He could feel his fingers faintly drumming.
A yellow dragonfly lit in his ear.
He smiled.

Ad-land puzzle

Is she wearing underpants, is the first question, of course, and while we can't tell for sure I suppose the answer must be no, and then we have to ask is the bath water dripping off her crotch onto her ankle-bones, and when she finally hangs up and walks away will there be a damp spot on the carpet?

To make any headway we have to explore the scenario. Let's imagine a little chart, or a little set of questions, with answers, and evidence to support the answers.

Was she taking a bath, or just washing her hair?

I think we have to agree that she was indulging in a full-blown bath, because of the bottle of body lotion standing on the carpet beside her. She wouldn't be using it on her hair.

Has she indeed washed her hair yet? Of course. It's wet.

Did the phone call interrupt her, whereupon she grabbed the robe and rushed out, or was she done, did she belt the robe carefully and saunter out to place the call herself? Her feet are dry.

She's got the body lotion. She wouldn't have brought it if she'd rushed out.

Who is she talking to?

Maybe she ran out of hot water in the bath, and she's calling Union Gas. But her hand is coiled into the cord in an intense fashion: she must be talking about love. Maybe she brought the body lotion, called up her lover, and intended to have at herself while she talked to him.

It's a touch-tone dial.

It's an expensive bathrobe, carpet, an expensive pair of knees.

Here's what I think. She finished her bath, dried, put on her robe, the phone rang. She sauntered out, picking up the lotion on her way, and answered on the fifth ring.

It's Jacob. He wants her to go to Connecticut for the weekend. She's undecided. It's not an ethical question, she's been sleeping with him for months, but something about the sentimental unreality of a weekend in Connecticut is suddenly too much for her. She realizes that for Jacob she's only a spare-time fantasy. She'd like to see him scrub a floor, or clean his fingernails. When she's with him, she forgets about that. She becomes the cream puff on the plush leatherette of his car seat, and they zoom off in the quadrophonic sound.

Vegetable lust

He couldn't keep away from them. God knows he'd tried. He began, as a matter of fact, at the far side of the bed. But that didn't last. As the days lengthened, the nights grew warmer, the skipping ropes and marbles came out, he found it increasingly difficult to restrain himself, and he began to inch closer.

Excuse me, mind if I just ... ah, that's better, thank you.

The rest of the carrots were quite satisfied to stay put. They sank themselves deep down into the ground, drank whenever they could, and discussed the playoffs. He tried to join them. But with the Habs out he just didn't care. It was anybody's cup, as far as he was concerned.

And all the time he could feel them there, three rows over, globular, succulent, becoming firmer and plumper with each passing day.

Every night he waited, until the other carrots were sunk into their salad dreams, and then he inched, roothair by roothair, earthworm by earthworm, closer.

The night he got close enough to actually hear their breathing slumber he could hardly contain himself. And

---

when they woke, first thing, and began to murmur sleepily to themselves under their blanket of glistening dew,
his lust knew no bounds.

At last he was as close as he could get to them, without attracting the gardener's attention and getting himself weeded out. Their plump red bodies burgeoned
under his eyes, as their leaves stretched and turned to
follow the passage of the sun.

He was beside himself. That night he couldn't sleep.
The coy radishes, curled into each other like nymphets at
a pyjama party, quietly giggled themselves to sleep.

He stood there, rooted into his row, his clump of
leaves aching up at the stars. At last he slept, but woke
instantly from a nightmare about a blender. His scream
awakened the radish nearest to him, the juiciest of the
bunch. Frowsled with sleep, she looked at him in alarm.

He couldn't stand it any longer. Symmetry be damned,
he thought. Gardeners be damned. It's now or never.

He plunged across the damp dark earth towards her
waiting flesh.

Symmetry

There are two of them. Sisters, probably, cousins perhaps, but turned out of the same craftsman's workshop. Two women, in their fifties, with grey shingled hair. Large, tall women. Just coming off the up escalator in Westmount Mall. Seven o'clock, the early evening summer sun coming through the skylight.

The shingled haircuts are striking, but unpleasantly so.

These two sisters could handle a canoe as well as any man when they were fifteen, sixteen. Now they live in adjacent houses, with husbands and families. They shop together for patio furniture.

Their shoulders are stiff. Canoeing shoulders gone wrong from lack of loving.

The only thing I can think, walking along behind them, absorbed with their perfect shingled salt and pepper haircuts, their shaved necks, is that they look like a couple of walking condoms. Tight, I mean. Packed in. Rubbery. They turn out casseroles for christenings and funerals with the same competence that they used to flip a canoe up over their heads.

When their sons come home five minutes after curfew, they ground them. If they come home drunk they belt them with a leather belt. Down in the recreation room.

While they walk through the mall, towards Eaton's, on the lookout for patio furniture, their dishwashers are churning and spitting back home in their kitchens.

No need to think of them sharing a room in a retirement home. They'll die, both of them, in their early sixties. An operation gone wrong—gall bladder, hysterectomy—or a car accident, an inebriated husband, after the last child's wedding, wheeling out onto a dark wet highway in front of a truck.

Every fall, for a week, the husbands batch it and the women drive down to Kentucky. They stay in Motels, go for walks after dinner with dark-coloured cardigans over their shoulders. Then they drive back.

The husbands, left alone, sit up late on one of the patios, drinking rye and ginger ale. They listen to the scrape of their lawn chairs on the flagstones. Talk about power tools. They think about the gap they're in. The TV dinners, instead of the casseroles. They wonder, each of them, what it would be like to have someone softer, fluffier, more pliant in their beds, but they don't mention it aloud.

Instead, they say, 'Well, wonder where the girls are tonight?'

Fixer

He was always there: a wisp of smoke, a flashing coattail, the smell of burnt rubber. Faustus in the garden, the abortionist, the pimp, you see what ballpark this little pigeon I'm riding is hovering over.

Fixer. Actually, he was a bus driver, with long sand-coloured sideburns. He swallowed a lot. His Adam's apple bounced. Tendons in his forearms tightened up when he pulled the lever to open the door.

Glancing up, glancing out, glancing back. Three panes of glass: two mirrors and the windshield. He always seemed to be on that one route, none of us remembers anybody else ever driving that bus, but he must have slept sometime, musn't he?

Those sideburns were remembered in bars, in hospitals, at the train depot, they seemed to leave an after-image of themselves all over town, like racks of plastic Groucho Marx noses and eyeglasses.

One woman saw them on a man flipping through the porn in the back room at the secondhand bookstore.

Another one looked up as she knelt at the altar to

receive the host, and there they were, sliding up the sleeve of a cassock.

Somebody else saw them on her baby, momentarily, through a cloud of dusting powder.

Georgie Palgrave found a set of the sideburns on the dirt under the swings in the schoolyard at Our Lady Immaculate, and he actually picked them up and put them in his pocket, but they were gone by the time he got home. Lucky for him, too, he thought, feeling for them as he went up the front steps, because he had a suspicious mother. She went through all their pockets: his, and his dad's, and his two older brothers'.

The sideburns were gone when he got home, but so was his mother. She vanished, out of their lives, out of their memories, there wasn't a time the four of them couldn't remember eating standing up, around the pot on the stove, forks in one hand, slices of bread in the other.

They never saw her again, and were the happier for it, but we remember her as the lady with the pink print dress and the grubby handbag who sat just behind the side door on the Fixer's bus. Scarcely a time we were on that bus, when she wasn't there. In fact, never. She didn't speak aloud, just looked around, sharply, and disapproved.

The Fixer had a gap in his teeth. He whistled through it. Spit through it, sometimes, at the terminal shed. Couple of the kids from Edgeworth said he showed them once a trick he could do: he set the butt end of a firecracker into that gap, and lit it, and let it go off there, bang, stuck right in between his teeth. Never stopped grinning.

A matter of perspective

What if you took Snoopy and tossed him under the edge of a steamroller, where it was parked at night by the vacant lot, and then in the morning it rolled over him? He'd be flat, there'd be a depression in the soft gravel, there'd be no mark on the steamroller, the driver wouldn't even know it had happened, nobody'd be watching, it's that early in the morning.

I suppose we should clarify whether we're talking about the real Snoopy, or a real dog, named after him, or some kid's stuffed animal. Is this a sodden, rag-eared kapok facsimile, or the golden mean of Snoopyness vanishing from the world?

In any case, how does this differ from a bug dying against a windshield? Are there bug mommies and daddies, bug godfathers, bug doting aunties, who will take out In Memoriam space on the obituary pages in bug newspapers to grieve over the bug death on the windshield?

Were it an elephant, rather than Snoopy, the driver of the steamroller *would* notice. Is notoriety, public grieving, attention of any sort all a matter of size?

If a steamroller were to flatten the Earth there wouldn't be any watchers. The Muzak of the spheres would go on and on and on.

Water-colour barn

Well, it's on the wall. It behooves me to say *some*thing.
Not that I don't *like* it, don't get me wrong. But does it
inspire me?

It's full of knotholes. They come from slicing fresh-
killed trees into boards, the saw blade showing no mercy
on arms and legs. Then the knotholes (i.e., thin sections
of arm and leg) get spread randomly around. Into barn
walls, for instance.

I use the term 'section' as they do in the Pathology lab.
They take a suspect slab of something from a guy who's
bought the biscuit anyway, so he won't be needing it, and
then they embed it in paraffin, and harden the paraffin,
and then take sections. Or, the verb, they section it. That
means slicing it off like meat loaf, into the thickness of a
single cell. The sections go on glass slides, and then they
melt the paraffin off. Students get the sections too thick,
get carried away cranking the handle on the slicer, forget to watch what they're doing. Wreck it all. So they
have to go get another chunk of something —it's okay, the
guy's dead—and some more paraffin and start all over.

Mornings, on my 8:00 A.M. run to the mail slots, I look in there and five or six Pathologists are happily cranking away, talking about 'Three's Company.'

It's right across from the Gross Room. That's also part of Pathology. I won't go into what they do in there, but they keep having to get the plumbers up because their drains plug.

Why am I pursuing this hard-edged carnality? I could just as easily have gone for poignancy, the abandoned barn, the cruel passing of time. I could have said that the painting reminds me of Floral, Saskatchewan, birthplace of Gordie Howe. A grain elevator, and a white wooden house, prairie. It makes me sad, thinking about his quiet home, the frail house and huge sky, with all his lifetime records long since toppled by the big 99.

Limpet

Tonight's writing is regulated by Seiko.
And they're off.

What about the Immanence of Christ, anyway? God
with Us, Emmanuel.

Do I really want him around, smirking in the corner?
Grinning knowingly at everything I do? I rack my brains
trying to offend him—pick my nose, holler smut about
his mother—and he just goes on *loving* me with his large
kind drippy eyes.

Yea, though I walk through the valley of the shadow of
death, there he is on the verandah, clipping his toenails.

The more I tell him to Fuck Off the more he smiles.

I'll tell you where it bothers me most. That spot on my
back, just between my shoulder-blades. The bit you can
only reach with a backbrush. That's where he likes to settle, and he settles in like a limpet. Where he knows I can't
get at him. Sometimes I wake up, 4:00 A.M., and feel his

weight there. The sleeping Christ, like a balled-up hedge-hog, oblivious.

Just when I think I've had it, when I think THIS HAS GOT TO STOP, he goes out and buys a watermelon, or offers to massage my feet. His sense of timing is impeccable.

If only he wouldn't smile all the time. If only he'd cut his finger, or contract a head cold.

It's got so I don't know what's him and what's me. If I cleared him out, poured the magic potion on him that made him shrivel up and disappear, I'm afraid I'd be missing a foot, or a kidney. I can't tell us apart.

But Seiko tells us our twenty minutes is up. Our race is run.

This has been the story of the turtle, folks. The hare's been there for hours, had a sauna, had the Virgin Mary, had another sauna, now he's talking over forming a syndicate with the Holy Spirit, to market commercial fertilizer made out of dove droppings.

God bless America.

Down to work

Rippling rills, fly casts, NEVER MIND these sylvan images, let's gut the bastard and fry him up. Butter, polyunsaturates, goose grease, who cares? Fry him, eat him, spit the bones into the underbrush.

We gotta keep our strength up. It's a hard cruel world we live in.

Little boys trying to drown even littler boys in swimming pools. Stolen underwear.

Long distance birds so addled they forget where they're going.

Footprints on the moon.

There was this guy my dad used to tell me about, had a cornea transplant, and he was so calm cool and collected, so centred, they didn't have to sandbag his head afterwards. He just lay there, didn't move his head a fraction of an inch for six weeks.

You know what's wrong with that story? What about night-time? What about gnashing his teeth and fighting dragons? What about wet dreams and falling down the long throat of a rabbit hole?

Maybe they sandbagged his head at night. Just at night. When the nurses took out the flowers and brought in the juice and the drugs, they sandbagged his head.

There. We got that one straightened out. It's been bothering me for years. I'd think about the story, and then wonder about night-time. But now, spit-spot, out of the chaos that surrounds us, I've invented a nurse in rubber-soled shoes who wheels the sandbags in at night on a cart.

Okay. That one's taken care of. It's not for nothing that we wolfed down this half-gutted undercooked fish.

What's next?

Genetic screwups

Clear through a hazy cloud of rancid underwear the one single Mohawk pine spiked up a cockroach's asshole to oblivion.

More netherlandish sharks popped playfully in the rancid deep. Mouldering leaves flashed cornucopiae of albumen and metabolites.

Helter-skelter skipping feet of bobby sox ran through the acid rain.

The oboe, the knife-blade oboe, cut the bread-loaf halving falling away like parted walleyed breasts. The last of the Mohicans farted, and was answered by a rumble of thunder from deep in the hills.

At six, they sat down to table, three at a side, the grandparents, bibs tucked beneath their chins, propped at the ends.

The setting sun toyed with their silvery hair.

A bird flew past.

A tampon flew past.

A 747 flew past.

The teapot rattled on its silver tray.

The grandmother took up three Flintstone vitamins, one after another, and drove them deftly into her nose.

The table folded down the centre, flapped its wings, and flew away in pursuit of the tampon.

Then ostriches strolled.

Can we get there by candlelight?

How *many* miles to Babylon?

The second-last Mohican did an M.A. in Physical Education on skin pigmentation and its effects on the respiratory system.

The third-last Mohican went WeeWeeWee all the way home.

Under the bed, with the dust-bunnies, old socks, used condoms, flügelhorns and expired charge cards, the first Mohican sat eating crackers and peanut butter and playing pocket pool.

The dolphins had the answer.

But they never mentioned it to anybody, and now they've forgotten it. I asked one, the great-uncle-once-removed-dolphin with the knitted cap.

Honey, I addressed him, what's the answer?

It's not anything, he said. But if you *want* it to be something, it's a chicken.

Seven empty chairs

When I first looked at them they didn't seem at all sinister. Just seven empty wooden garden chairs, weathered, the slatted kind, fanned at the top, drawing in like a narrow waist at the seat. They were on the cottage porch, on top of the cliff, facing west to the sunset over the lake. Empty.

I sat on the cliff-edge, with the chairs on the porch behind me, and watched the golden sun sink into the water. Two children and a dog frisked on the beach below. It was darker down there. Grey and brown.

I turned once to look at the chairs. Seven, in a row. Their symmetrical backs polished with use, glinting in the sun. The ball of sun orange in one of the cottage windows.

It was then, just as I turned to look back at the lake, that I felt a catch in my throat, a sudden clutch. The chairs, behind me, formed an accumulated concentrated weight between my shoulder-blades. They wanted to push me off the edge of the cliff, stomach-first, breast-first, into the plexiglass edge of the world, into God.

I leaped up and ran back to the porch. Sat down on the

wooden floor, back firmly against the cottage door, and looked at the chairs. They were strung out in a line beside me. Four on one side, three on the other.

They turned, in unison, ever so gracefully, looked at me, and then turned back to face the lake.

One was playing solitaire. Another was smoking. A puff of wind lifted a six of clubs and dropped it on my leg. It slipped off and fell through a crack in the porch floor.

I pressed my back against the cottage wall, but I could feel it being torn away, by grasping wooden fingers. I was sliding forward. The chairs were murmuring.

I knew it was them or me. The one who was smoking dropped an inch of glowing ash on my shoulder.

I jammed my heels behind one of the chairs, began to push it towards the edge of the porch. It tumbled off, corner-first, into the flower bed. I crawled back, caught another, flung it over, and then the next. I had them all, finally, upended into the dirt.

I knew I had to hurry. I'd broken their force field, but only temporarily. While they were toppled, unsymmetrical, was my only chance. I leaped off the porch, grabbed a chair in two hands, and sailed it off the edge of the cliff. Back for the next. Each one was harder to lift. But I managed. Two, three, four ...

Number five I had to shove across the grass. It cut huge gouges into the dirt. When it toppled it took stones and small shrubs with it.

The sixth was even worse. I pried it over with an iron poker I found by the fire pit. Heavier than anything I'd ever lifted.

The last chair, the seventh, had dug itself a hole down into the earth. I beat it with the poker, felt it wincing, and grabbed its arm with both hands. I tugged, pulled, braced myself, got it going, it picked up speed, I wrapped my legs around it and the two of us, the chair and I, sailed into the sunset.

Ossuary

It looks like one of those word scrambles in the paper, the letters waiting to pop neatly into the right order, like a set of cartoon teeth.

sauryos. yassoru.

Yossarian's sombrero swept across the estuary.

In dreams of hot sandy countries, prados, richly woven blankets, Latin lovers, we always forget to mention the sordid details. Where to spit, when we've finished brushing our teeth. Camel shit on our sandals.

Armpits, swamps, however you sort that word, rearrange it, diddle the dipthongs, it comes down heavy like a monsoon. Hitchhiking across North Africa, never mind the return ticket from Gatwick to Montreal stuffed down your brassiere, you have to first *get* to Gatwick, and that means hitchhiking across North Africa. Screw all the linebackers in the CFL and we'll give you an ice-cream cone.

That air rifle, popping off next door, p-funk, it's a new acquisition, never into the hands of that little fucker nor his cretinous friends would I put even a watergun,

I imagine myself over there tomorrow, speaking to the parents, Nothing that comes from the Mouth of that Gun must cross my Property; behaving like a self-righteous prick.

I can't get out of my life, I can't get out of my life, where will I spit this ever-expanding mouthful of camel shit?

ossuary: a receptacle, popular in seventeenth-century Bohemia, made usually of brass, richly ornate, into which depressed matrons, in the early evenings of the dog days of summer, upon hearing nearby gunfire, expectorate camel droppings.

ossuarian: having the characteristics of or pertaining to any receptacle into which shit may be spit.

ossuator: shit-spitter.

ossuate: in the blessed state of having spit shit.

The view from below

First of all, there's the Setting. I'm in here with a group of Spanish or South American women. It's tiled, there's a kind of urinal-bathhouse quality to it, like Colville's woman in the tub, or that upstairs bathroom in the bed-and-breakfast near Hampstead Heath.

What I see, what the dream has me focus on is one corner of the floor and a bit of wall. It's a rectangular tub arrangement, the front two sides not formed by the walls are only a couple of inches high. Like the shower stalls at a municipal swimming pool.

Floating in this rectangular corner pool are corpses. We, the women and I, have come to sit out the night with our dead. The corpses are either the real thing embalmed in some peculiar way, or models of the deceased.

The youngest is a baby; his mother keeps fretting at him. It's just his head, but solid, as if it were done in plastic, or marzipan. Rigid and stylized, like the lid of a fast-food container. Quite a shiny surface. The corpses lurch and roll as if they were bobbing in water, but there is no water.

After the baby, the second youngest is mine. It's my

110

son, about two years old. Similarly plasticized, but he has more of a body. The legs and feet are minimal, turned up against the torso and moulded in whatever the matrix is. A spray of flowers lies against him—glads, or roses, funerary flowers—also moulded in, the blooms by his head. It's like those Victorian greeting cards, where the flowers are incorporated into the overall design. He's bent backwards, so that the entire object wants most to float belly up, the head and vestigial feet submerged. Although submerged is wrong, remember, because they're floating in air.

I keep prodding at him, trying to flip him around so I can see his face, but he keeps bobbing away from me.

The adult corpses, two or three of them, are less active. They roll quietly against the wall edges, in the backwash from my son and the baby-head, both of whom are lurching around quite actively.

The other women, the baby's mother and the wives or girlfriends of the adult corpses, are mourning in what appears to be the wonted manner for whatever country this is. Grief spills from them in tears, wails, sighs. They clutch each other, cover their faces with swatches of their clothing, then fling themselves away and stagger about the room. The mother of the baby darts in beside me where I'm kneeling at the edge, and prods the head so it bobs violently, causing waves that make the others jostle like boats moored at a marina.

Remember, still, no water.

I'm unable to let myself grieve. There's one tiny chamber, in the bee-eyed centre of my brain, reinforced like a bunker, where I know that I know that his death is total devastation. Pain. The ending of the world. When the rest of my mind plays over this a riptide of nausea clutches in my throat. I know that's in there, but I can't let myself confront it and join with the other women in their open grief. I think of the time when I'll be away from all this, back in Canada, alone, and I know that when I finally open that chamber I won't survive it. It will be immediate white killing heat, like an atomic blast.

Meanwhile, I stand, or I kneel at the edge, watching my son. We're together in this country where death must be treated in this way, where custom requires that he go through this plasticization and dry-matrix bobbing, and I have to stick with him. I have to do it this way or not at all. I know that he knows that I am here.

The secret chamber of my mind tells me that this scene is unconscionable horror, but I ignore it, refuse to do anything, even weep. The women are companionable, include me as one of them, don't appear surprised by my evident lack of emotion.

The room connects to a room, other rooms. Up a couple of steps, a small hall and then a doorway lead to a bar where the males are drinking, singing, performing their accustomed part of the wake. Laughter, shouting, music, clinking glasses, the noises come through sporadically. The mourning women are attached to various of these men. I am attached to no one except this grotesque remnant of my son.

The Action of the dream is sewage. A vent-like opening connects the corpses' rectangular basin to a washroom. Urine, turds, used sanitary napkins float through from the toilets, wash in on the corpses. I'm revolted, want to grab my son and run, but I know that the law requires that I leave him here in the mess, that if I pull him out I will be shot.

———————

The following night, I'm newly arrived at a detainment house. The Venue could be North American, but the Cast has an international flavour. Guerillas, Gestapo. It's German and South American — nothing oriental.

The house is three or four stories, and has the feel of a commune. Lots of windows, plenty of morning light, we're free to walk about, but there are soldiers with carbines posted at the outside doors.

I've been here one night, my bed was in the attic, now I've come down to a second-floor kitchen to eat breakfast.

The two horrific things:

I've not been taken notice of yet by the authorities —no grilling, etc., but I know, as I watch them walk past, up or down stairs, occupied with their own operations, that what's in store for me are sexual atrocities. I look at myself as I sit at the kitchen table — my arms, my feet — I feel my hair tucked in a bun at the back of my neck, and I'm conscious of how much I don't want to be violated. I'm not ready for it. I think about a grey-carpeted living-room, in the twilight, with a stereo and a record cabinet, bookshelves. I don't panic. I'm very quiet. But I can feel it coming: my body turning to meat, the pain.

The two guys sitting at the breakfast table with me are lean and tired. They've been detained here for several days. As we chat, I discover that they're brothers. They bring me up to date on atrocities perpetrated by our captors, outside, before any of us were brought here. The chief one of these is the death of their father, who was strung up to the back of a kitchen chair by one testicle. The brothers were forced to watch him die.

The whole thing is somewhat like a summer camp. There's some question of bringing out our dirty clothes so they can be sent to the laundry.

You know these dreams, you were there when they occurred; I don't know how you can still calmly ask, Where is your novel? Why do you persist in writing these cluttered ill-fitting scraps, that assemble like too many coffee mugs on the drainboard?

Burnout

There's just too much going on. Splayed elbows, for one, not to mention the late frost. Heavy preoccupation with making money. Imminent death of immediate family members. The castration of the dog.

Loose talk about dongs, wangs, noodles, peters, hoses, cocks, tools, sweet potatoes, flaming sizzlers.

The pen is mightier than the sword. Dip yer quill in my ink-pot, wouldja baby?

There's entirely too much MOR radio. Bad songs from the seventies. And as if the death of Christ Himself wasn't enough, there's Sarah Vaughan and Harold Ballard and Greta Garbo. What a trio they'll make, pounding on St. Peter's gate.

And then we're expected to focus on this picture. Which is itself way too full. A bronze naked statuette on the mantel, eyeing itself in a mirror. A clock. A meerschaum pipe, a wind-up toy locomotive, to scale, six innuendos and a pair of false eyelashes.

And, foregrounded, a lady with a large head and a wedding ring, reading. Dressed in black. White lace at collar and cuffs. A look of intelligent self-conscious intensity that women of her era were forced to adopt to defend their brains. Nowadays you can see smart women lying around on the street. They're a dime a dozen. Back then, they wore black, softened by lace, sat quietly, and looked intense.

Just above her left collar-bone, its head peeping up through the lace, is a millipede. She's felt him there, tickling, but she thinks it's a downdraft from the fireplace rustling the lace itself. Doesn't think too much about it, because she's concentrating, posing for the picture.

I'd bring her along, have her discover it, throw the book in panic over her head and rush from the room, screaming, but I don't have the time.

Last weekend the neighbour over the back cut down all his trees, and ran up a Union Jack on a new flagpole. Does he think he's claiming territory for the king? Is he angry at his wife? Has he gone, simply, quite mad?

You see, there's just too much to consider. Is the most effective flea spray finally being marketed this year with a pump, so we won't destroy the ozone?

Do the Korean Presbyterians all own variety stores and play the piano, or is my sample just too small?

What is the shelf-life of an innuendo? How long before it becomes dessicated, or begins to leak?

There's just too much going on.

The great northern migrant snot-picker and his dog

I'll put him on the outskirts of Timmins, sitting slumped at the lunch counter of a place that sells camping supplies and fishing licenses. Ice. Brightly-feathered lures fanned out on a piece of cardboard. He's on his second cup of coffee. The dog's lying at his feet, nose resting across the toe of one of his scuffed hiking boots.

I know he has stories to tell. Or a past, anyway, that would become stories if it were listened to. Incidents with some point or shape that would isolate themselves out of the long matrix of hitchhiking and sunburn, afternoons of draft beer. And the dog, too, thumping his heavy tail now and again on the wooden floor as the man shifts his weight on the counter stool and talks to the teenage waitress. The dog has a past of gravel in his paws, the scent of gopher, wet sloppy ditchwater, wind.

But who am I to want these stories, to imagine that I have a right to them? Right now, at ten-twenty of a Thursday morning, on the outskirts of Timmins, I can put myself at a table by the window and drink my own coffee, watch him idly pick his nose, and rub the snot onto the leg of his jeans, while the dog lifts his head, and then sighs, and lays it down again on the boot.

That's all that's possible. I don't want the man's life for my own, or the dog's life, although it would be nice to scratch the dog's head, and feel his rough fur. But he's not my dog.

What I have, here, is my own cup of coffee, my car keys, and the gritty nuisance of a pen that wants to put down words.

Last memory two

Chewing. Chewing and chewing and chewing. Chewing
and chewing and chewing and chewing and chewing.
Then the drooling.
Just a small bit of drooling.
The very tiniest silver thread of drooling.
Then a slurp.
One abrupt slooping slurp.
A doze. A little slack-jawed balloon of a doze.
A snort. A start.
Chewing. Chewing and chewing and chewing.
Dreaming.
Dragonflies on the riverbank. Lazy dozing dragonfly
riverbank, seven angels chasing the dragonflies, seven
godheads chasing the angels, seven leviathans chasing
the godheads chasing the angels chasing the dragonflies.
On the riverbank.
Farting. Letting her rip, into the air.
Chewing, Goddammit! Chewing and chewing.
Get this chewing all done before suppertime. Supper
they make me drink with a straw. My jaws too tired from

my afternoon chewing.

Chewing up tree trunks and bus tickets and pebbles and nipples and ducks. Duck feathers duck bones duck bladders duck spleens, duck feet duck tongues duck aprons duck spatulas duck ovens. Chewing.

Chewing in my chair chewing in my bath chewing in my bed chewing up a dogsled spitting out whalebones spit 'em into heaven, hot like rivets, getting there before me, LOOK OUT he's coming, here come his whalebones, DUCK those rivets, the damn fool's on his way.

from the
Dragonfly Notebook

The Basic Equipment:

The tools of the trade. (Warp, weft, spinnakers, pur-
fling, bits and bytes, soffits and fasciae, Phillips and
Robertson.) The tackle.

Here, in the case of these dragonflies, it's very simple:
pliers, telephone wire and glue.

I bought the glue three months ago, right after the
woman at work gave me the first Harley-Davidson package. I was on a break with her, in the cafeteria, when they
still allowed smoking. I'd run out, she had two left, she
said, so she hauled out this stunning package. Shiny.
Black, with the gold feathered bird.

We each had one. I almost passed out. Very strong.
Dazed and reeling, I asked her for the package. I got the
glue on the way home from work.

No, I told the girl, I'm not going to sniff it, here's a
testimonial from my doctor, my religious advisor, and the
lady three doors down who grows prize gerania.

Yes, I said, I will use it in a well-ventilated room. Just gimme the damn stuff.

It was as bad as buying rubbing alcohol. For that, I've finally had a little card printed.

SORE NECK MUSCLES
I WILL NOT DRINK IT
HAVE A NICE DAY

The pliers I bought just this afternoon, from an old family-business hardware store. On the way home, I passed the front of the yellow brick house, and there was the girl in her cherry-red coat, playing with her little sister and a toboggan. Whew.

The telephone wire has been around forever. It's copper, very thin, coated in colourful plastic; a bundle of wires together make a cable. Enough of it was once given to me by a retired Bell executive to do Home Crafts, at the present rate of consumption, for eleven hundred years.

This Bell executive, when he went to do jigsaw puzzles, sorted the pieces by shape and lined them up:

4 knobs

3 knobs, 1 hole

2 knobs, 2 holes,
opposite

2 knobs, 2 holes,
adjacent

1 knob, 3 holes

4 holes

edge: 2 knobs,
inner hole

edge: 2 knobs,
inner knob

edge: 1 knob, right,
inner hole

edge: 1 knob, right,
inner knob

edge: 1 knob, left,
inner hole

edge: 1 knob, left,
inner knob

edge: 2 holes,
inner knob

edge: 2 holes,
inner hole

(NNE by NE
NNE
ENE by NE
ENE)

corner: 2 knobs

corner: 2 holes

corner: 1 knob,
1 hole

corner: alternate
1 knob, 1 hole

miscellaneous
(one example
of many)

Edgar and his puzzles, we said fondly.

Shortly before his death, he confessed that he sorted the pieces by shape because he was colour-blind.

Place

Oh, I don't know. Where *are* we all? Outside this dark window is the lane I walk up every morning on the way to work. There's a kid's treehouse in one backyard. And down a few houses, where a man just died (I once taught his granddaughter how to play the recorder), an angry girl stomps around the garden saying, 'What do they *do?* Just walk *past* this garbage? Every fucking morning? I've had it, George. I've just had it. I'm at the end of my tether.'

And next door to that, a woman with eleven cats, who's saving one Agatha Christie to read on her deathbed.

And down at the very corner, last house on the right before you hit the street, a marriage came apart, lurched drunkenly around, and then thwok! it stuck together again. Meanwhile the oldest son flunked out of most of the private schools in the province.

Two babysitters in another house, one of them played the double bass in the grade eight string orchestra. His older brother, thin and lean, gleaming teeth, glossy hair, I wanted to send the kids out to the party, and stay home with him myself.

Out of the lane and onto the road, straight across, a music inspector for the Public Board. I was in a classroom one time, singing with a bunch of kids, and he popped in for a surprise inspection. The teacher blanched, muttered at me, 'Don't let them sing any of the songs they like. He hates it if they look like they're having fun.' So I taught them 'Oh where, and oh where, has my bonnie laddie gone?' from the *High Roads to Singing Book Three*. Strictly curriculum, and mournful as they come. When he left we got back to *The monkey he was drunk / he sat on the elephant's trunk.*

Up the road itself, a house where we went for dinner one night, and I immediately got into a fight with the hostess. About how important it was that a kid should keep his socks clean. She tilted her clean positive chin at me as only a nurse can do, and I saw red.

A few houses down from there, my boss. He stopped on the sidewalk one day to show me a dragonfly that had chosen to light on his outstretched hand.

Inside here, inside this dark window, a child's painting taped to the wall.

 it says.

I am here.

The Little Glass Girl
and the Little Glass Boy
go to New York

They were wrapped in grey cloaks, featherlight, and they strode through the outskirts hand in hand in that silent time between fog and smog. Death strode with them, coughing.

They'd been walking all night. The blisters on the boy's feet were hurting. His boots were new, made of stiff elephant leather. The girl, whose footwear was softer, walked a pace ahead, picking the easiest way through the cobblestones. Death brought up the rear, only his shadow touching the roadway. Scuttle crabs froze solid as he passed, under their corners of rock.

The boy and girl were hungry. Their pack was empty. Death had celery secreted here and there in the voluminous billows of his cloak, but he didn't share it with them.

At last, after miles of rough and broken pavement, the girl found what she was looking for. A black staircase, leading up, between two buildings, into the morning mist. The boy didn't have the strength to climb, but she went ahead, tugging at his hand, and he put one foot painfully on the bottom step. Death, despite himself, was growing fond of these two, so he assisted from behind, balancing the boy's rump in his bony palm.

As they climbed higher, their feet clanging on the metal, the sky grew brighter. The boy was getting dizzy. Eleven steps, a landing, a quarter turn, eleven steps, a landing ...

The girl said, we're almost there. Death tightened his bony grip on the boy's rump.

Finally, they reached the top. They came through the clouds, and their heads broke into sunshine.

Death, unprepared, fizzled and disappeared, leaving behind some stalks of celery at the boy's feet.

Panting, chewing celery, they gazed out over the city.

The right

August Kleinzahler, on the corner of a letter about something else, a postscript, an afterthought, said 'Great story, Jean! Women aren't supposed to write that way.'

What, what, what way?

I took the story, again, read it, again, what way? Does he merely mean that I call a horse's anus an asshole? Could it be simply that?

The way we're supposed to simper and take sherry, when what we'd prefer is scotch? And we're not supposed to stand around in the kitchen at parties, leaning against the fridge, and swap stories?

Surely, August knows better than that. But *what* way?

I buried the story in a pile of other women's stories. Read through from the top of the pile. Came upon it, quite by accident, my sensibilities cleared, neutral ...

Maybe it's the word orgasm.

But no, other women say orgasm in print.

I was driving out of a lumberyard one time, onto a busy four-lane road, in a summer cloudburst, there were four of us in the car, myself, my two children, my mother, our breathing was steaming up the windows, I couldn't see through the steam, the sheets of rain, the splashing of traffic, I was in some haste because my mother, a woman of unpredictable digestion, had an overpowering urge to find a bathroom.

I wasn't wanting to turn right, but to dart directly across the road into a Tim Horton's, where we'd find a john. So I was waiting for a four-lane gap. But I couldn't see. The driver behind me was infuriated. Honking, he finally pulled around me on my left, screaming ASS-HOLE! as he passed, tore out into the traffic.

My children and I convulsed, my mother appalled.

The question arose, over doughnuts, my mother safely into the ladies', did he mistake me through the misted window for a guy? Do men call women assholes?

My daughter took the question back to school with her, to people twenty years younger than myself. They did a survey. Most said no. Except to women they know well, and then only fondly. But not in anger. Bitch is still the big winner, for anger.

Why can't we be assholes, too? Come on, let me be an asshole.

Cows

I wish I was an owner of cows, so I could smack them on the flank. I had a big dog once. I used to smack *him* on the flank. That was as near as I ever got. He'd look around, bored, and say whatcha doin', asshole?

Sometimes it's fun to hit the carpet. It has to be the right kind, though.

Some trees are good.

The best thing to smack on the flank, short of a cow, which is my ideal although I've never tried it, is a Henry Moore sculpture. You can't do the ones indoors at the AGO because the guards glare, but there's the one right outside on the street corner. You can step right inside that one, just walk right in there and smack away until the streetcar comes. There's a double thing happens, you get the slap of your hand, and then the big bronze boom, like the Liberty Bell.

Very nice, very gratifying.

And you can stare down the people waiting for taxis and the streetcar, because this is a Piece of Public Art. And you are a Piece of Public. You and this art were meant for each other. You were brought together, in fact, at the government's expense. So you can eyeball them directly, with your open face hanging out, and raise your flat hand and smack that old Henry Moore flank like there was no tomorrow.

But a cow flank, now.

You see the thing is, the cows would enjoy it. They know, inside, down in their little warm masticating cowy cuddy hearts, that their exteriors are made for smacking. They spend their whole lives, trudging from one field to another, swishing flies, chomping down raw grass and spitting it up and chomping it down again, just WAITING for somebody like me to come along and smack them.

I would be, were I independently wealthy, an itinerant cow-smacker. I would spread contentment from one field to the next. I wouldn't be paid, I couldn't be hired, I'd smack only those cows I chose to smack, those ones I could sense would really enjoy it. I'd stay away from the big centralized farms. I'd be famous, but as a phantom is famous. I'd stay right off Letterman.

A farmer would come out one morning to the barnyard to find his cows all dreamy, sloped against the barn wall, and he'd be able to tell by their grins that I'd been there in the night, smacking away.

But by then I'd be long gone, eating my bit of bread and cheese, washing it down with the bubbling water of a clear brook.

When I tired of smacking cows, I would move on to tickling fish. On that delicate spot, just behind the gill. Only I would be able to make them giggle. Only I would be able to hear them giggle. A solitary pleasure.

I'd get one promising fish, and train him to hold his breath for minutes at a time, and then I'd combine these two most human of pleasures. I'd smack a cow's flank with the fish. There'd be that flatness, but a wetness too. The dripping fish, thwacking onto the cow flank.

The fish would giggle, the cow would grin, and then I'd run back to the stream and pop the fish back in before he ran out of breath.

The cow would graze on over the hillside with the fish-shaped smack-print drying in the sunshine, and the fish would bury his nose in the silty brook-bottom and remember the feel of his fins paddling the empty air.

And I would disappear down the country road, whistling into the mist.

Stoop

There are so many ways to go. Enumerating them would be one of the ways. But I guess I'll opt for Einstein's eyebrows, because they contain all the rest.

There's a porch, for one thing. The particular kind of porch that is a stoop, is one where good slow unarticulated things can happen. Where it's so safe not to be able to figure out your income tax that you can come up with $E=mc^2$.

Walking home from the Uplands, in Wales; from the grocery store, in good Canadian English: 'buggy-shops' the kid calls it. One kid in the pushchair, one walking beside, a plastic bucket swung on the handle filled with groceries, the nut comes off the end of one of the axles, and rolls away, and there I am, stuck. I can't carry the baby and the groceries and the pushchair, the baby's tired, starting to whine, the walking kid has to pee. An old lady comes along, a neighbour, eighty-four, she's stooped, deaf as a post, wants to know what I'm looking for. She's the straw that breaks the camel's back. I want to grab her little old throat and tear her head off. But she's so gentle, so stooped; she looks, with her old doggy face, so like the Karsh photograph of Einstein that I explain to her, kindly but shouting because she's deaf, about the missing buggy nut. She paddles off the way we came.

Talking to her has calmed me down. I organize the groceries, the kid, the baby, the pushchair, make them all sit in a row on the curb. I sit down in the street in front of them, stare them down until we get back the porch-stoop of stoop, until they're all smiling.

The kid turns her head, looks down the sidewalk, spies the little lady three blocks away, waving her cane over her head. Tiny frantic insect in a shoebox peep show.

She's got the nut, of course. We collect ourselves, I wave at her, she stands and waits, we make it down the sidewalk, the kid says, 'She's getting bigger and bigger'; she waits, I know she'd wait all day if she had to, she's that kind of stoop, safe, until we get to her, take the nut, reassemble the buggy, hook on the grocery bucket, stick in the baby, take the walking kid's hand, hug the old lady with the other arm, watch her large-eyed Einstein-eyed smile spread over her old, worn, gentle face, and turn towards home.

Love gifts

A child, a chubby child.

A lock of hair.

Three wriggling worms.

A pablum sneeze.

A requiem mass.

Fire.

Ten Hail Marys.

Money by wire, branch to branch, to pay the phone bill.

Elephant shit.

Triple-word scores.

Seventeen crab-apples, packed into your underpants.

The perfect translation.

An open-throated white shirt, looming out of the barnyard at dusk.

Socks in a pail, soaking in Javex.

The lapping of milk.

Car tires hissing on wet pavement.

Bubble gum cards.

Alphabetization.

Pounding arpeggios.

Meal-tickets.

Beaverslaps.

The bunny with the best battery, drumming till dawn.

Probing fingers, counting the vertebrae.

Running on the shore with a blue airmail letter.

Rug hooking.

Camel lips.

Green shadows under a bathtub.

A walking bass.

This incredible wooden bird, standing guard by the fireplace, yellow hair on end, startled out of all conscience by the pattern in the carpet.

Lamplight.

Tractor seats.

Hailstones.

Bluegrass.

Tumbleweed.

Microscopy.

Flatfish.

Plums.

Raft

This little child would wait all day. I've promised her an
ocean voyage I won't be able to deliver, and I know she'd
sit here until the sun goes down, still believing in me.

The dog is faithful too, dear old Brébeuf, but then
that's what dogs are for. They lollop about, doling out
faithfulness like the old Queen on Boxing Day.

We've got the log raft, and our sun-hats, we've packed
a little lunch, and here we are mired in the sand, unable
to launch. I'm too frail, and she's too small. It's all still
jolly, she doesn't suspect yet that we won't be moving, I
guess it's up to me to weave another strand of plot around
us, tailor-make the story to fit the events.

Something in me resists that, now. I'm tired, I guess.
I've woven the texture of so many lives, kept so many
boats afloat. Elderberry turnovers on a rainy day, when
the picnic was spoiled. Thunder is the gods' bowling
alley. Even with Harry, in the Crash, who needs money,
I said, we've got love.

They all believed me, swam through my stories into
lives of their own.

And now here I am, stuck on a raft I can't float with a sweet seamless child and an affable oafish dog, and there are no more stories to spin. The basket's empty. I'm going to die soon, and none of my stories is strong enough to see me through that. Nor anyone else's stories. I never did like Jesus; heaven's a bore.

The little girl stands up, jumps down off the raft, ankle deep in water, the dog's ears snap forward, waiting for her to hand him his script, 'Granny,' she says, 'I'm sea-sick. We must leave this shaky boat. Take my hand and we'll see if we can walk to the sun.'

Men need a dancebelt

They *gotta* have 'em. They grab 'em, and whup 'em around, and beat onto tree stumps and go huegh huegh. Then they soak their feets. Couple times, every afternoon they soak their feets.

Don't dry 'em off, just walk around they dry okay.

Then they eat. Celery, lotsa times. Some steak. Jam. They get their jam in tins. Keep it in the shed.

Then they grab them dancebelts, womp 'em around some. Sometimes they break windows with the buckle end, but mostly they wallop stumps.

Then they call up. Do a lotta callin' up. Then they walk on over, and bunch. Take along some jam, and they all soak their feet together. Pickin' out the tadpoles, from between each other's toes. Spittin' jam seeds.

Feet good and clean, they womp them dancebelts some more.

If somebody's brought a book along, they put it up in the cleft of a tree, and fill it full of bullet holes. If nobody's thought to bring a book, they get the catalogue.

Help each other out at funerals, too. Stand around.

One time one a them's kid got a fever, they all brought over them dancebelts, leant 'em to the kid. Piled 'em all up on the foot of his bed. He died anyway, but them dancebelts all piled up made a pretty sight.

Don't wump 'em much, of a morning. Just listenin' to doors slam, then, and waitin' fer Fred. Not that he comes, regular, but they do a lot of waiting. Couple of 'em catch flies with their tongues. Fast, like frogs. Suck the pulp and spit out the wings.

The rest a them stick to jam.

Fred's got a car. And a job, even if he don't do it regular. Up and down, on the days he does come. Everybody waits, and then stops spittin' when they watch him go by.

That's it. Just stop spittin'. Nothin' like hello Fred.

After he's gone they sit a while longer, and then start whompin' stumps with them dancebelts.

Last Christmas at home

He works, occasionally, on weekends, for a caterer. In the
lull between fall weddings and Christmas, his hair's
grown so long that yesterday the new vice-principal, mis-
taking him for a stoner, wouldn't believe him when he
explained why he missed an English class. Tonight he has
to work a Christmas party, is required to look snappy, so
I give him a haircut. He sits on a stool in the living-room
in his dress pants and shiny shoes, bare shoulders
wrapped in a towel, watching football on TV.

Sucking up the clippings with the vacuum, I notice
that they're not so blond or curly as the first time I cut it
when he was a baby. He goes off to a mirror to check it
out, wanders back to see the completion of the play.
Unaware of his return, I take him one in the kidney with
my vacuuming elbow. We both start, and shout. Scare
each other.

Two A.M., when he gets home, he sits on the piano
bench in his white shirt and black bow tie, eating cold
Champagne Chicken left over from the party, talking on
the phone to his friend who's staying up all night to finish

The Brothers Karamazov. He tells him about one of the guests, a drunken doctor who couldn't stop eating the paté. Speculates on what his puke will look like tomorrow.

Then he says, 'Santa Claus is training wheels for Jesus' (the first line of a hit country and western song I'll probably never write). Goes on to explain how if a kid believes a fat man coming down a chimney, it's an easy jump to a thin one dying on a cross. And when he realizes they were lying, he stops believing everything.

What have I told him that he'll have to unlearn? Not that one, certainly, I never was much for Santa, but there must be other untruths lurking, waiting to nick him when somebody else cuts his hair.

Extremis

It's my turn, goddammit, it's my fucking turn, so it behooves me to clamber partway up the glabrous edges of this bung-hole of despair and put something on paper.

Shut the door in the face of the stray kitten, prop up the dying decapitated sunflower head, and begin.

I could just talk about the frayed lawn chair, with its faded patchwork cushion; and how sad and empty it makes me feel to read about travellers, in their second-rate hotel rooms, downing shots of brandy from their clouded toothglasses. The blinding glare of sunlight in the Alps, or the traffic on the Autobahn.

Or how I lie awake nights, picturing crashes, arrests; composing conversations in police stations — should I be the sneering intellectual, the disdainful theorist; or the welling-eyed mother, my pyjama bottoms flaring out under the hems of my blue jeans? Clutching my handbag. Dropping a Tampax on the counter in an attempt to find my driver's license, to identify myself.

Yes, I am this boy's mother.

No, he is not in the habit of being in trouble with the

law. A character witness: he danced with the girl with the limp at the grade six sock-hop.

And when they let him out—do they accept VISA for bail?—he's sustained injuries which are not congruent with a fall from a bicycle. I drive him directly to the nearest hospital.

This is Canada. Policemen are our friends.

This is Canada. Policemen are beating up our Native people.

On the way back from the bathroom I check the rack. His helmet's there. He's been upstairs asleep during this entire scenario.

I've had my hair in pigtails for three days. Once in my youth, on the main street of Parry Sound, an American pointed me out to his little son. Look. There's one of them now.

I imagine being surrounded by a rock-flinging mob in the parking lot of the Sherwood Forest Mall. Honour requires that I don't tell them I'm not an Indian. Rather a descendant of a German-Swiss farmer and a French Huguenot, both fleeing from religious persecution. Met mid-Atlantic on the boat *Myrtilla* in the year 1765.

I engage the mob in a Socratic dialogue. The noontime sun shimmering on the parked cars. One by one they are illuminated by logic, covered in shame. The rocks drop from their hands. They disperse, as crowds do in the media. Melt away. I'm left alone with the yellow Goodwill pick-up box.

In real life, the immediate tedium of day-to-day, unre-
lieved by anxiety or dream, the stray kitten plays with the
ends of my pigtails. I talk on the phone and suddenly
there he is at my throat, claws out, a pigtail staked by each
paw to my collar-bones.

What? says my caller. Are you all right?

Yes, I say, they've only pulled out another fingernail,
it's okay. So far I'm managing fairly well. My eyelids are
gone, but the sky has been overcast. The media are a bit
bothersome, they keep tramping in the fire and yelping.

Microphones in the face of the mother in Halifax harbour, watching her son climb aboard one of our washtub
warships headed for the Middle East.

How do you feel at this moment, he asks her.

She's flown down from tree-lined suburban Ottawa
for this departure, this time last year he was point guard
for his high school basketball team, how the hell does he
think she feels, the asshole?

They keep asking me the same thing, how do you feel,
how do you feel, the flames have singed off the fluted
pyjama-legs, now they're licking at my finely articulated
ankle-bones, and I don't know how I feel, I could use a
Coke with some ice, I suppose, but other than that ...

Why am I being required to pay? I didn't bring the
smallpox, I wasn't the matron of a residential school, I
interned no one, in a camp of any size.

Just what have I done?

One on one

They're not saying anything. They just sit on chairs. Sometimes one of them will sneeze, or scratch.

If something comes up, they react to it. I mean, if a bright shaft of sunlight beads down through the transom, they might both squint a little. Or if they hear rain on the roof, their eyes travel up towards the ceiling momentarily, and then down again.

But they don't remark on it. They never remark on it.

They're not shy with each other, it's not that. They're not trying to avoid noticing that they both squint at the sunlight. They do notice it, but no remark passes between them.

And no body English.

They just sit on their chairs.

I don't mean to give the impression that they're like a couple of cats. Flicking their whiskers around in tandem in response to every stimulus. Quite the contrary. Sometimes a sunbeam comes through the transom and one of them won't squint at all.

Their thoughts go off in quite separate ways.

One of them might think about playing Rummoli, or eating hamburgers, or walking along the river with the dog.

And at the same time the other one might be remembering how boring that stretch of 401 is between Woodstock and Kitchener.

Every now and then she thinks about what it would be like to fall asleep with her arms wrapped around him, but at that exact instant he may simply be recalling that flying squirrels don't actually fly, but merely launch themselves on long soaring leaps.

So they go on sitting on their chairs. Every few minutes they get that much older.

He might speculate on falling asleep in her arms, but by this time she is trying to remember, in succession, the main themes from the slow movements of the six Brandenburg Concerti.

On days when the transom is closed and it doesn't rain, there's very little connection between them at all.

Once, for a moment or two, they both thought about fish. But for her it was the dark liquid eye of a pike, deep in a Muskoka river, while he was grilling salmon.

They go on sitting on their chairs.

Not saying anything.

Negative space

That's me, at the end of the dock, in that severe wooden chair, all chopped into triangles and glued back together. The negative space of the summers of our youth.

September, without fail, I feel for my wedding ring; and how many years has it been now, four, five? Rub my fingers against each other while I'm walking down the street, and think did I leave the cats in or out, are the children in their beds, rub and rub and then remember, oh yes, no ring.

I'm tied into this chair, Picasso-fragments glued together, I'm not drowning, not in the depths, those aren't my deck shoes, I'm not down searching out my past in the underwater caves, I'm in the chair, on the dock, stuck; see, that tiny triangle is an eyeball, there's a breast just above the sloping canvas seat, my long shin-bone is that upper stretch.

Hard for the parts to communicate, dismembered and fixed as they are into this random pattern.

There's no automatic signal for it to be over, no school bell, no beeper, no end of autumn, I'll sit here all winter,

I guess, until I figure it out, I've given up on the magic fish that will leap golden from the water and blow a tiny silver bugle at me. No such fish will appear. No.

I'll just be in this chair. Dismembered. Getting so accustomed to the fragmented state that I think it's normal. A breast epoxied smuck just above my left ear? Of course! How else would you have it? Where's *your* breast? What? There? Beside the other one? On the *front?* Good heavens.

Down some hill on some island in some Mediterranean country some small girl with some stuff in a grocery bag runs pell-mell past some chalk-white house and hurtles into her own front courtyard and stumbles, falls, skins her knee on the cobblestone, and cries and cries.

That might do it.

See you

Off he goes into the Saturday suppertime rain, the last of a string of downtown encounters; I've talked the whole day away on street corners.

Smoking at the bus stop, watching the blackbirds rim the windows.

Rain.

Sometimes the downtown buildings feel like my bones. A warm southerly blows among them. The trains go in and out my armpits, in and out my nose-holes.

I can see everything at once.

Last memory three

Small phunt walkin by. D'ya see im? Nope? Just here a
minit ago! Blue. Wet feet. Trunk swingin. He was tryna
sneeze er somthin. Funny noise. Hfn hfn. Lookin fer
somthin. Barbie Doll, er onea them harpoons.

Offerda feed im. Shook his head. Hell of a hurry. Next
time, he says. Yeah, like he comes by here every day.
Sure. Never seenim bfor in muh life. And he says 'next
time,' like three tomorrow be too early? Shall I bring the
buns? Or woudja rawther meet ina park?

Wish youda seen im. Wish I knew wadeze lookin fer.
Wish Ida gone with im. Wish youda come earlier, er heda
come later, er Ida thought ta get a ride on his trunk. Wish
there wuz *some*pn elsn ese goddamn blue tracks. He's not
here, I'm not there, *you're* here but not *then*, with him, with
us, when you think we coulda *all* been goin off, blue
tracks, lookin fer that Barbie or that *har*poon.

Woulda found er, too, either one. And you coulda
picked up somea that good bacon on yer way over. Either
way, Barbie er the harpoon, we'da had a real good time,
us two an the phunt.

Ice fishin, now that's cold work. Far cry from plungin under the covers with Barbie. But either way, like I say, woulda been okay.

But look, now, the tracksr dryin, the dust'll be blowin over em soon, I'll be sittin down, *you'll* be goin off, phunt's gone, evrthin's gone.

Damn.

from the
Dragonfly Notebook

The scraps of paper accumulate throughout this dark hoarding winter. They abut, collide, crawl out to cover the wall. They hum to each other, flap and feed, nurture themselves in this little room, this kitchen. Closely observed by the restless predatory cats.

Clouds cross the sky in the darkness, driven by a strong easterly from Quebec; they head out over the lakes towards the prairies and the whining harmonicas.

Cecil, out at the depot, turns the radio up full blast and puts his feet up on the boss's desk. He ignores the screaming printout. What he don't know won't hurt him. Out beyond the woodlots, above the riverbed, two freights meet head on and buckle into a culvert.

Between the clouds, a blistering full moon. Black branches of the maples dip and glide, dip and glide.

Over on Maitland, Lucy lies flat on her back, watches the band of moonlight creep slowly up from her toes, along the counterpane. When it gets to ...

there … she knows she'll die. She can't say crotch, she can't even think crotch; … there … is as specific as she can get. She watches the silver death-band inch up past her knees.

Mrs. Morrison can't get her baby to stop coughing. It annoys the dog who rolls and sighs, drums his foot, sleeps, wakes to more coughing; the baby's head is asweat with fever, the curls damp and clinging.

The unrelenting headlamp moon burns its way across the sky. Fresh banks of wind-driven cloud billow in, pile up, snuff it out.

Blessed dark.

Lucy lets herself breathe, unclenches her fist, rolls over on her side. Maybe next time.

In the smoking west, the night is still clear. The harmonica whines, coyotes answer.

A breeze from the open window lifts the paper scraps; they flutter on their stick pins. The cats are beside themselves. They poise, hunch up, and fling themselves against the wall.

———

There's a patch of bare grass under the neighbour's picnic table. It's opened up like a moist surprising armpit, surrounded by snow. Creatures too small to be seen by the naked eye are perhaps turning over in the unexpected warmth, murmuring their equivalent of *mmm, yes, that feels good.*

In here, inside the window, I refuse to be fooled. I know it's only the beginning of March, I know it will be weeks yet before I can go spinning along the riverbank. I look at this collection of backyards, the jumble of branch and shadow spreading against the backs of houses. Window frame, cornice, the slope of roof, an empty grape arbour, a leaning toolshed. Long spans of weather-treated impenetrable privacy fence. From here I can see right over them into gardens where, at the moment, nothing private is taking place.

Except for the inexorable slump of grey snow, melting into the dark earth, opening up this frowsled patch of bare grass under the picnic table, where the tiny creatures awaken, turn slowly into the warmth, and say *yes, now, yes, we're ready.*

Born in Vancouver in 1943, Jean McKay has lived in Calgary, Toronto, Saskatoon, Swansea, Wales, Sault Ste. Marie and London, Ontario. She was co-editor, with Stan Dragland, of *BRICK a journal of reviews* from 1977 to 1987. Several of her short stories have appeared in Canadian literary magazines. Her autobiographical novel *Gone to Grass* was published by Coach House Press in 1983 and won the Gerald Lampert award for prose that year. She now lives in London where she is a medical secretary. She's currently working on a new book of short stories.

Editor for the Press: Sarah Sheard
Cover Design: Stephanie Power / Reactor
Cover Photo: Michael Ondaatje
Printed in Canada

Coach House Press
401 (rear) Huron Street
Toronto, Canada
M5S 2G5